THE MAN
WHO WAS
MURDERED TWICE

THE MAN
WHO WAS
MURDERED TWICE

by

ROBERT H. LEITFRED

RAMBLE HOUSE

2014

ISBN 13: 978-1-60543-792-7

TO THE MEMORY OF
STEPHEN CHALMERS

Preparation: Gavin L. O'Keefe and Fender Tucker

Cover Art © 2014 Gavin L. O'Keefe

CHAPTER I

LAND OF PROMISE

THE PANAMA LINER *COMMANCHE*, red-funneled, broad of beam, and jammed with tourists, curved around the starboard side of the breakwater lighthouse, straightened its course, and with engines turning over at half speed, steamed importantly through the oily waters of the coastal city harbor towards its Pacific berth.

Proudly arrogant, it ignored snorting tugs, odorous fishing boats, and tramp steamers cargoed with lumber, bricks and oil.

It has been said, with more malice than charity, that this Pacific coastal city was striving desperately to be metropolitan, and was failing miserably. It has also been said that it was nothing more than a hick town suffering with growing pains.

All this is far from the truth. The coastal city is as old as the Conquistadors, as rambling as New York's lower East Side.

Above all things, this coastal city never did things by halves. So it could not fail miserably. If it failed at all, it would fail with flags of all nations flying, bands blaring, searchlights stabbing the night sky, and airplanes writing the word in letters of smoke miles long above her California shores.

Its harbor, curiously enough, was thirty miles or more away from the city proper which would seem to speak rather well for the astuteness of its city fathers. The ships of the world fouled its waters, unloaded their merchandise and departed. The battle wagons of the Pacific, sleek gray cruisers, gunboats, battleships and plane-carriers, disgorged, regularly, all the hard-bitten sailors and marines of the fleet—in fact these same gentlemen occasionally took the city apart to see what made it tick.

All this was not apparent to the eager-eyed passengers on the coast-wise ship, *Commanche,* as the oil tanks, lumber piles, fish debaucheries and scavenger boats floated past the *Commanche*'s jutting prow.

The coastal city was insidious. It sort of fastened itself to one like a mild attack of hives. It made everybody itch to be bigger and better than everybody else. Religions and cults flourished in its sunshine like green bay trees. Slot machines tinkled. Nickels rattled. Punch-boards gave out useless numbers. People cheated on cash registers here as elsewhere.

And scandal, murder and rape blushed in the news headlines, was marvelled at and forgotten. The coastal city was no miserable failure, it was a miserable success.

Forward on the main deck of the *Commanche* stood a lean, dark, dissolute young man, negligent in appearance and cold sober. Ned Anderson was darker than the rest of the passengers because of a prolonged sojourn in parts of Ethiopia.

He had existed comfortably among the natives. He had existed not so comfortably among the invaders. Boredom made him ill along with assorted fevers. Now he was on his way home to the coastal city to renew his interest in the affairs of an estate which kept him in pampered if not bored ease.

But several things had happened during Ned Anderson's long sojourn among Haile's former subjects. During his absence of two years on the Dark Continent and other continents as well, his estate had been purged systematically and completely. In other words he had been rather unkindly but thoroughly robbed of his entire fortune.

Had he known the exact status of his financial resources at the moment the red-funneled *Commanche* was entering the harbor, he would have been less kindly disposed towards the world in general, and coastal city in particular. Being young, ignorant of his loss, and proud of his birthplace, he looked forward to his homecoming as something in the nature of an event. He hummed tunelessly as he surveyed all these familiar landmarks.

"Well," remarked a stout passenger, squinting from the shoreward sights to the tanned face of Ned Anderson. "I can't hand this place much. Far as I know it might be New Jersey on a sunny morning—allowing the sun was shining, y'understand. Same kind of boats. Same scum on the water. Same stink. Same . . ."

Ned Anderson yawned. "My good fellow," he observed, cheerfully, "have you ever seen any of the ports in Africa? You haven't. I can tell that at a glance. They're terrible. Hot, oppressive, and when the sun gets just right, that Red Sea is *red*—not blue or pink, but downright red."

"I heard you, Mister, the first time you said red. But I ain't interested in Africa. I'm talking about America. Listen. I come from New Jersey to see California, and I came like you through the Panama Canal. And I ain't seen anything yet on this trip but a lot of riff-raff of this and that. By God, I came out here to see something grand and magnificent. And what do I see? Ask me!"

"All right," said Anderson. "What do you see?"

The stout man squinted and blew his nose. "A lot of water, docks, lumber piles and boats. Listen here. I live in Hoboken. I got all this scenery in my back yard, as you might say. I work in a brewery. I've been saving my money for this vacation. And when I start to figure what this trip is setting me back, I wish I had banked my money and hauled a rocking chair out on my back porch. Could have seen the same sights from there and not spent a nickel. Bah! California here I come. It's a racket."

"Brother," said Anderson, staring dreamily shoreward. "Your philosophy is sound, but your logic, rotten. What you need is a drink. Come to my cabin. There's still time before this old hulk cramps to her berth."

Eastward across the state, by a matter of some three hundred miles, a bunch of coastal city cops cluttered the main highways leading into California from Nevada and Arizona. The idea behind this cluttering was somewhat involved, but its actual execution was simple.

Bums must be kept out, turned back. People with lucre, jobs and homes were welcomed, stickers placed on their windshields, cars searched for bags of forbidden fruit, license numbers checked, and the fortunate ones were allowed to enter the interior.

The cops, red of face, husky, trimly uniformed, did an excellent job in handling their disagreeable task. The Press damned them with equal partiality. Headlines ran: COSSACKS COERCE COMING CITIZENS. POLICE PURGE BORDER BUMS. And the poor cops sweated and wished they were back home where it wasn't so damned hot.

Two boys in a ramshackle Ford braked to a stop at the barricade. They came from the wilderness of dust and parched fields. Their hopes were high, their cash reserve low. Cold meat for the cops.

"All right, son," said Sergeant Breen, not unkindly, to the lad behind the wheel. "Where do you think you're going?"

"Santa Barbara."

"Yeah? Why Santa Barbara?"

"We got jobs there."

"Got anything to prove it?"

"No."

"How long since you had your last meal?"

"Yesterday morning."

"Then you must be broke. I'm sorry, lads. But I'll have to turn you back. Those are my orders. This state is already over-crowded, and our relief agencies have just about gone insane trying to figure how everybody's to be housed and fed. Hi, Terry. Take these two lads over to the Desert Inn, fill their bellies with all they can eat and have it charged to me. Then see that they roll eastward towards the Colorado River Bridge." He turned. "Who's next?" His eyes lighted on a gleaming, low-slung, red Auburn with New York license plates. Behind the wheel crouched a man with a pale, boyish face. Beside him sat a hard-visaged man, wide of mouth, thick lips, and a hoarse, guttural voice. He grinned at the police sergeant, took a fat roll of bills from his pocket, and peeled off a twenty.

"We're fixed with plenty of dough, Sergeant," he said, extending the money out the open window. "Okay to push on?"

Sergeant Breen nodded. "Okay with me. Let him through, boys."

The gleaming car swung past the barricade and went dusting down the hot, desert road.

Sergeant Breen looked at the twenty. He called to another cop. "Just to keep the record clear, McBurney. One of them birds—they looked like a couple of hoods to me—slipped me this twenty. Take it over to Dago Joe's Inn and have him put it against the food bill we're paying for out of our own pockets. This job is the nuts. Here I'm just married hardly a week—and stuck out here in the Styx! All right, who's next?"

He passed through two cars of well known make, then stopped a noisy truck. "Ha," he chortled. "And where to, Mr. McClusky?"

"Oi, such a policeman," said the driver, a red-bearded son of Israel. "I'm goink to Lonk Beach, y'understand. See, in de back. Tires, old metal, old magazines and nusspapers."

"That's fine," said Sergeant Breen. "But you're a hell of a long ways from Long Beach. Lemme see your license." He squinted at the car license wrapped around the steering column, examined the driving license, grunted and returned the small card to its owner. "Drive on, McClusky."

The red-bearded son of Israel drove on into the dust clouds created by the cars that went before. Business slacked off for a moment. Then came a man on foot, his face red with heat and moist with perspiration. He looked vexed.

"Just a moment," called out Sergeant Breen. "Where are you headed?"

"To the coastal city," said the man. "I started out with a car. I was robbed of the car and most of my money which was in the side pocket of the door."

"Them's sad words, stranger," grinned the sergeant. "I've heard them plenty. There must be a lot of thieves working the highways bordering California. Tough I calls it. What's your name?"

"Edward Smith. I'm a law clerk. And I have good reasons for coming to California. I've got a job."

"That's fine, Mr. Smith. And who's this job with?"

Edward Smith took a folded sheet of paper from his pocket. "Here's the offer of work from . . ."

"I can read plenty good," said Breen, taking the letter from Smith's hand, noticing as he did so the missing joint on the little finger of the man's right hand. The heading was that of an investment broker with offices in the coastal city. The letter ran:

Dear Mr. Smith: I have examined your credentials and found them satisfactory. Enclosed you will find a cashier's check for your expenses west. Will expect you not later than the 15th inst.

Yours very truly,
James Gillespie

Sergeant Breen returned the letter to its owner. "Looks legal to me, Mr. Smith. I guess I can take a chance on you."

Edward Smith nodded. "Thanks, officer. How far is the city from here?"

"Roughly three hundred miles. But if you walk it, it'll seem like three thousand. Why don't you take a bus? There'll be one going through here after supper tonight."

The face of Edward Smith broke into a wan smile.

"That's a good idea, officer. I think I'll wait for it. I'm somewhat fatigued with walking."

If Edward Smith was a good law clerk, his training did not end there. He was also a good poker player. With that sure instinct of men who know their way around, he found a poker game in the town and a seat among the players.

He had five dollars when he sat down. The session lasted three hours. When Edward Smith got up from the table he still had his five dollars, and seventy besides.

He smiled wanly on the other gentlemen, apologized for having to quit the game. Quit the game, ate a substantial supper at Dago Joe's Desert Inn, stepped onto a transcontinental motor bus, and was whisked across the state over desert and mountains, and into the fastness of the sleeping coastal city.

In an apartment at the Belvedere Arms, two men discussed a radiogram dispatched from the *Commanche*. The message read:

GILLESPIE SECURITY BROKERAGE COMPANY. ARRIVING WEDNESDAY. STAYING AT COMMODORE TEMPORARILY. SEND ME NEW CHECKBOOK.

NED ANDERSON

James Gillespie, slender, innocuous in appearance, clean-shaven and outwardly nervous, flipped the message towards the other man.

"He's here, Baron. Registered at the Commodore this afternoon. And I needn't tell you I'm worried sick. The last time I heard from him he expected to be away another six months—time enough to get everything taken care of, and all risks eliminated."

George Baron, counselor at law, bail-bond expert, fixer extraordinary, and a man of parts, smiled suavely. There was about this attorney an aura of respectable urbanity. His cheekbones were high, prominent. Eyes, wide-spaced. Hair slightly gray about the temples and matched by a trim, gray mustache. He could exude a warm, personal charm on occasion. His reputation was brilliant, but spotted. He got along.

"I trust," said George Baron, "that you sent him the new checkbook. Because if you didn't . . ."

"But I did," said Gillespie. "What else could I do?"

"Nothing. But cheer up. That fellow Smith will be here, maybe tonight. When I sent the check I wrote a letter on your stationery. I also have his picture. Startling, Gillespie—the resemblance between you."

A frown creased Gillespie's forehead. "I'll be glad when this business is finished. The girl suspects that everything is not quite right. It was that confounded check. She saw it, but didn't say anything, but I saw a queer look in her eyes."

"We've got a good man following her. She can't do anything without our knowledge."

"You think we can safely trust this man?"

"As much as anybody can be trusted."

"Just the same I'm worried. I have a feeling that . . ."

"You should have thought of all of this at the time you lost all your own money and started to think about how easy it would be to make use of Anderson's account."

"Oh, how was I to know? Things looked right for a killing in the market. I thought I saw some good chances to clean up. Anderson was far away, drunk probably. And I had the power of attorney. Well, I figured wrong. The Wall Street boys cleaned me . . ."

"Not quite, Gillespie. There's still a little matter of about two hundred thousand in cash and negotiable securities. The agreement was, I believe, that we would split this amount evenly provided I arranged things as originally planned."

James Gillespie admitted this fact. "That was the agreement, but it seems somewhat involved. Isn't there any other way out?"

"None that would provide the maximum of safety. Want to call the deal off? Want to handle the thing yourself? Maybe it's on your mind to skip the country and leave your attorney holding the sack as it were?"

"Nothing like that, Baron. Everything's in your hands. Just the same, when the hue and cry goes out from the police and sheriff's offices, I'm the man they'll be looking for. So the quicker you get things fixed, the easier I'm going to feel about my future."

George Baron nodded gravely. "Of course. I understand your grievance, and I can't blame you for being—shall we say, nervous. But give me time. My outside talent is on the way from New York. When they've done their work, I'll pay them off, and they'll go back east. It's really going to be quite simple—and effective."

"It had better be," growled Gillespie. "Anderson may be a sap in a lot of ways, but there's no telling what he'll do if he becomes the least bit suspicious and asks for an immediate accounting. It would make things difficult to handle."

"I don't believe," said Baron, lighting a panatela and inhaling pleasantly, "that there'll be any trouble from that direction. After all, Ned Anderson isn't overly endowed with gray matter. Just sit tight and leave everything to me. Now pour me a small Vermouth, then I'll be leaving."

Gillespie, his hand not quite steady, reached for a tall, narrow bottle. "I don't mind being accidentally killed, Baron, just so long as the police don't . . ."

"I'll handle the police," promised George Baron, setting down his empty glass and getting up. "There'll be no trouble about the identification. Get hold of yourself. Hell, accidents are happening every day. The investigation and medical examiner's report will be simple routine."

Gillespie nodded drearily as the door closed behind the departing attorney's back. But there was a glazed, hunted look in his eyes. Never had he wholly trusted George Baron. He hadn't trusted him when he had taken out a certain insurance policy that was, in a way, an unusual form of protection.

A thinnish smile parted his lips. Even Baron didn't know about the terms of this particular policy.

CHAPTER II

A NIGHT CALLER

THE MAN WHO MIGHT or might not give these two highly es-
teemable gentlemen cause for worry was, at this particular
moment, deep in his cups in a suite of rooms at the Commodore Hotel. Before him on a table littered with the remains of
a late supper were three jade-green bottles—two of them
empty.

The eyes of Ned Anderson were sad. "It's no use," he told
the empty bottles. "Here I am home and bored to extinction.
California, here I come. Come? I'm here! Oh God, thirty
years old, lousy rich, and I'm as useless as a wart on a toad.
No guts, no ambition, nothing. Can't even get tight without
wanting to cry. What a man!"

Once more he filled his glass, sighed and drank moodily
without being in the least exhilarated. "If I was poor like
most of humanity," he reasoned, hopelessly, "I'd probably be
working in a ditch or sleeping in a gutter. But being rich I'm
forced to drink myself into it—which isn't so hot."

The buzz of the telephone broke in on his moody cogita-
tions. He regarded the instrument solemnly as he lifted the
receiver from its cradle.

"Hello," he said. "Who? Don't know her. Never heard the
name before . . . can't help it . . . I said . . . Listen, let's begin
all over again. Miss Laird, you said. I still insist that I don't
know her. Oh! All right. Send her up. Wait. Don't send her
up. I'll come down. Tell her to wait in the lounge." He hung
up.

"Now who the Devil," he asked himself, "is Miss Laird?"

Miss Laird, it developed on his meeting her in the lounge,
was a towhead. She had a wide, humorous mouth, and deep

violet eyes. She might have been called pretty by her mother. But by any other standards she was definitely—not.

Ned Anderson bowed politely and guided her to a deep chair in a secluded corner of the lounge. His eyes studied her casually, half-appraisingly.

"So you're Ned Anderson?" she said. "Please sit down opposite me. I haven't any designs on you. I simply want to talk to you and tell you what a stupid, wasteful and utterly incompetent person you are." Ned Anderson exhibited mild interest and sat down. "Ah!" he sighed. "You restore my confidence in human nature. A truthful and observing person. May I smoke? Thanks. And you? Too bad." He lighted a cigarette and leaned back in his chair. "Please proceed with the indictment."

Miss Laird's violet eyes became thoughtful. "I don't suppose you know me, Mr. Anderson, like I know you."

"Skip that part, Miss Laird. Who are you?"

"I'm that *vl* that's always at the bottom of Mr. Gillespie's letters to you."

Anderson took Gillespie's last communication from his pocket, and there, sure enough, following Gillespie's initials, were two letters in small type—v and l. He had never noticed them before. He was exhibiting more mild interest when he said: "V for violet?"

"Virginia."

"Virginia is much nicer. Southern hospitality, magnolia blossoms, horses, crinoline, hams . . ."

"You're not a serious person, Mr. Anderson," she broke in.

"Sorry. Frivolous is the word. By the way, how is Mr. Gillespie? I must look him up in the morning."

"You really plan to exert yourself that much?"

"Yes. I need the exercise."

"You're going to have all the exercise you want during the rest of your life. As a matter of fact, Mr. Anderson . . ."

"Call me Ned."

"As a matter of fact, Mr. Anderson, I have a feeling that you and I are shortly going to be looking for jobs."

"Odd," said Anderson. "I never thought of going to work before. Don't know what to say. I once had a lady friend who worked—in a department store. Wait! Don't interrupt me. She was a law student nights. Days she was a store detective. I liked her tremendously, but she couldn't see me at all."

He paused and rubbed out his cigarette in an ashtray. "You see how it is, Miss Laird. I'm talking just to hear the sound of my voice. As I just remarked, I've never given thought of going to work—that is, seriously."

"I've always worked," said Miss Laird, calmly. "Probably always will, so I'll get along somehow."

"That's fine. But perhaps I'm dense. Maybe there is something you said that somehow got by me. I'll admit I'm not overly bright, but at least I'm not altogether stupid."

"My mistake," said Miss Laird. "Before you left on your world tour, you gave Mr. Gillespie power of attorney. I hope you can recall this act without undue mental strain."

"Which means," said Anderson, "that my fortune . . .?"

"Is practically nil," finished Miss Laird. "It also means that Mr. Gillespie will close his office—that's where I lose my position—and depart for distant shores."

"You sure of all this, Miss Laird?"

"No, I'm not sure. After all, Mr. Gillespie is a capable executive and keeps part of his business to himself. I do know however, that he has lost tremendous sums of his own money in the stock market. I know also that his cash reserve has never been adequate enough to handle any such amounts as he has poured into Wall Street."

"Mere suppositions, Miss Laird."

"By mistake, Mr. Anderson, a canceled check for seventeen thousand dollars, signed by Gillespie against your cash account, was included in the cancelled checks sent through the account of office salaries and expenses. A bank mistake, but Mr. Gillespie was furious. He knows I saw the check, but he's never mentioned it."

"You think there were others?"

"I wouldn't know about that."

Ned Anderson was silent for a long time. Finally he said: "Katharine Cornell is at the Commodore Theatre in Shaw's St. Joan. I think I can get a pair of tickets for tomorrow night if you care to go."

Miss Laird's violet eyes were faintly quizzical. "I expected to see you blow up. I really did."

Ned Anderson smiled. "I've got a home in the foothills outside of town—in Los Gatos canyon. Quite a shack. All of twenty-one rooms, tennis court, swimming pool. Do I still own it, or does . . .?"

"I wouldn't know that either."

"I'd like to know," said Anderson, wistfully.

"Call the tax assessor's office. You can find out in five minutes. But you'll have to call in person at the bank where they have your account."

"About tomorrow night," asked Anderson. "Do we go?"

"By tomorrow night you'll be too sick for anything but a moving picture."

"I don't like pictures. I want to see a good play—especially Miss Cornell. The last time I saw her was in New York in the Barretts of . . ."

Miss Laird rose to her feet. "It's late. I must be going."

"Why did you come to me, Miss Laird, with all this?"

"I don't know, really, Mr. Gillespie is my employer, and I know that I owe him a certain allegiance. After all he paid me a good weekly salary. But . . ."

"But what?"

"If you must know, I had a certain contempt for you. Call it pity, it sounds better. I thought if you were warned, you might not be hurt quite as badly as you might be later on."

"Do you still feel the contempt . . ."

"No."

"Or pity?"

"You don't need anything I can give you," she told him.

An odd quirk turned up the corners of Ned Anderson's lips. He seemed detached and far away. "Did you know you were a person with considerable charm, Miss Laird?"

The violet eyes snapped. "Is that a line with you?"

"In a way—yes. A life-line. I'm afraid I'm going to need one. But whatever my faults, Miss Laird, and there are a lot of them, I have never been accused of saying one thing, and meaning another."

"Did I say . . .?"

Anderson shook his head. "No. You've been swell. Do we meet tomorrow night?"

Virginia Laird shook her head. "Please, Mr. Anderson. I know you mean to be nice." She smiled brightly. "But let's forget it. Shall we?"

"Just as you say. May I see you home?"

Again she shook her head. "I know my way around. And the trolley cars are still running." She extended a small hand.

Ned Anderson pressed it gently as if afraid of crushing it. "Good night," he said.

The bright smile was still on the girl's lips. "Good night," she echoed.

He watched her receding figure for a long second as it moved down the wide corridor towards a side street. Then something leaped into his mind. Something he must ask her. He frowned and started after her small figure with long strides.

The telephone beside George Baron's bed shrilled impatiently. He took down the receiver.

"Listen," said a voice. "I'm in a booth at the Commodore."

"Go ahead," snapped Baron. "So what?"

"I followed the jane like you ordered. She came to this hotel, spoke to the clerk, then went into the lounge. A guy came down the elevator—Anderson, I'm pretty sure. They're in there talking together. She's telling him something. I couldn't get close enough to hear everything that was said, but I heard something about the bank making a mistake."

"I see, I see," said Baron. "Listen, Coughlin. Get back to the lounge and watch her. If she leaves alone, follow her and get her into a cab. You'll know how. Then bring her here."

"You mean to make a snatch?"

"You heard me."

"That's a big order in this state."

"Do exactly as I say. I'm not going to harm her. But I know she won't come of her own accord, and I've got to talk to her—tonight before anyone else gets to her."

"Okay," said the voice. The receiver at the other end clicked. Baron hung up, lighted a panatela, made certain his houseboy had left the building for the night, then switched on the light over the drive, and sat down to compose himself while he waited for Coughlin to arrive with Gillespie's secretary, Virginia Laird.

Irritable because this girl was bound to cause him trouble unless he closed her mouth, he closed his eyes and tried to plan how this was to be done intelligently, so that the suspicions of the girl's family would not be aroused.

As Virginia Laird pushed through the circular doors leading to the street, a man came up behind her, turned back the lapel of his coat, and motioned her to a taxi a short way down the street.

Ned Anderson, following some distance behind, saw him take her arm, saw her look rather wildly around, than start to shake her head. The man's hand gripped her arm. She started to protest and stiffened. He shoved her forward. Her heels slid across the concrete walk towards the cab door which the driver had opened.

Sensing trouble, Ned Anderson broke into a run. Her scream, muffled against the man's chest as he pulled her head down into the fold of his arm, was hardly audible in the din of night traffic. Still holding her tightly, he crowded into the cab's interior. The driver reached out his hand to shut the door.

At that moment Anderson reached the cab, knocked the fingers from the door's edge, and reached a long arm inside. Coughlin, handicapped with the struggling girl, snapped a short blow to Anderson's face.

Ned caught the blow on the cheek, but it did not stop him. He got hold of Coughlin's arm and yanked him from the cab. Then he swung hard—harder than he seemed capable of.

Coughlin staggered against the edge of the open door and sprawled back onto the fender.

"Hey, you!" shouted the hack driver, belligerently.

"Same for you," clipped Anderson, swinging the mate to the first blow into the hacker's face.

Virginia Laird emerged from the taxi, her face white, lips trembling. She went to Anderson. Got between him and Coughlin, who was rising to his feet. "Don't," she pleaded. "Let them go."

She pushed him back, her hands on his coat lapels. Anderson's eyes glittered as he watched Coughlin partly cover his face as he got back into the cab. The driver was already behind the wheel cramping the machine away from the curb.

Ned took her arm. There were two spots of color on his cheeks faintly visible beneath the tan from African sunlight. "You hurt?" he asked, reaching casually for a cigarette.

She shook her head and clung to his arm. "I thought for a moment," she said, "that I was going to smother when he held my face against his horrid coat."

"Mine wouldn't smother you. See, it's soft, woolly."

"Be serious, won't you? Tell me, was that man a detective?"

"Detective—private dick most likely, ordered to follow you, then kidnap you. Why? I don't know. Somebody's interested in you."

"Who could be interested in me?"

"That's what we'll have to find out." He had her by the arm and was leading her back into the hotel. "We'll go down to the cocktail room and have . . ."

"I can't. I have to get home."

Ned Anderson eyed her steadily for several moments before speaking. "You can't go home. Don't you suppose the man who wanted you kidnapped knows where you live. He'll try the same stunt again, and where will you be?"

Virginia Laird wiped her lips with a tiny handkerchief. "I really don't know. Nonsense. Who would want to kidnap me. I haven't any money, and no friends who have any. And

I'm sure my boss, Mr. Gillespie, would not consider me so valuable that . . ."

"Precisely, Miss Laird. I think you've placed your finger on the festering spot—Mr. Gillespie."

"Why, why, you don't think . . .?"

"I'm not thinking," said Anderson, examining his skinned knuckles. "I wish I had hit that fellow harder—both of them, for that matter."

"You hit them brutally hard. The sound of your fists striking their faces almost made me sick."

Ned took a possessive grip on the girl's arm and led her to a chair. "You're not going home. Call your mother if you want to. But you're not going home or to Gillespie's office until I've had an accounting with him."

"And when will that be?"

"Tomorrow morning—as soon as the banks open and I've checked on that house of mine I was telling you about."

"You seem to have developed a considerable amount of force since I first met you."

"No, I don't think so. Same old Ned Anderson, a little irked, sober and in need of a drink. Otherwise I haven't changed a bit. I still think you're beautiful . . ."

"Are you talking to me, or to all these people in the lobby?"

"I'm sorry," he spoke in lowered tones. "Will you marry me? That will quickly solve the problem, and . . ."

"I'm going home."

"But you haven't answered—listen, I'm proposing."

"Don't be silly. Why should I marry you?"

"I can only think of one reason."

"And that?"

"I like you."

Impulsively she reached out and patted the backs of his hands. "You're awfully nice, Mr. Anderson, even if you are an incompetent sort of a human being. It's been a thrilling evening—especially the abduction rescue. I'm dumb, I know, for not swooning in your arms and burying my fevered skin against that soft, woolly coat of yours."

He did not smile at her levity. He was worried by something he was only vaguely beginning to understand. "I'll take you home," he said.

"All right. But let's not be too serious about this. Call it mistaken identity. Somebody thought I was somebody else— an heiress with scads of money in all the banks."

"Let's call it that," said Ned. "Come."

They found a Yellow cab outside in the rank, got in and were whirled away through the soft night.

George Baron stopped his pacing as the phone jangled. He lifted the receiver. Coughlin's voice crackled from the receiver.

"Sorry, but the thing didn't jell. I had her in a cab, but Anderson butted in and jammed things up right on the street. Had to call it off. But I didn't lose sight of them. Later he took her home in a Yellow cab."

The lawyer's eyes narrowed. "Well, it can't be helped. That's all for tonight. Keep in touch with me. Dismiss the cab and pay off the driver—just in case."

"Okay."

Baron hung up, waited a few seconds, then lifted the receiver and called a number. A voice said: "Hello."

"Listen, Gillespie. It's the girl. She went to Anderson at the Commodore. I had her followed. Think she talked. Don't know for a certainty."

"I see," said the voice of Gillespie. "That's bad."

"Here's what you do in the morning. Make up a dummy package for her to bring to my office. Impress on her mind that the package is important, and is to be delivered to *me* personally. Understand. I won't be in the office, but here in my house. She's got to come here."

"But Baron, you aren't . . ."

"I said I wanted her to deliver the package to *me*. You tell her to come here in case I'm not at the office. She's something we hadn't figured on, and she'll have to be taken care of."

"Of course," said Gillespie, wearily. "Depend on me. Anything else to be done?"

"No. Sit tight. Anderson will be down to see you in the morning. Stall him off. Good night."

Both men hung up. Baron's eyes were hard and brittle. Gillespie's were frightened.

CHAPTER III

CLIENTS

THERE ARE, IN ALL LARGE CITIES, private detective agencies that have no connection whatever with the police. Some of these agencies are reputable, others shady. The private operators, taken from all walks of life, work for lawyers, gamblers, racketeers, department stores and manufacturing plants.

They also work for individuals. People in trouble, unwilling to seek police protection or aid, come to these agencies with their petty schemes, and for a fee, are helped or immersed into deeper trouble.

On the seventh floor of a building in coastal city's business district, one of these agencies had a suite of offices. The glass panel of the door was labeled:

SIMON CROLE
SPECIAL INVESTIGATOR

In the front office behind this door at her neat desk sat Etta, plump, bland and keen. On either side of the secretary's desk were two doors. One led to a small room usually occupied by Crole's operator, a singular individual known as Matt Ridley.

The other door led directly into Simon Crole's consulting office. The room contained chairs, a wardrobe, a couch covered with worn leather, and a heel-scarred desk.

The head of the agency, Simon Crole himself, sat behind the heel-scarred desk scanning a tabloid which featured the latest developments along California's eastern borders where the police were trying in vain to stem the tide of undesirables flowing into the promised land.

A big man, Simon Crole, with a certain feline grace in his every movement—and he was quite bald. Wrinkles slanted fanwise from the corners of his eyes. And his lips, whenever he smiled, twisted slightly out of line because of an ancient scar, creating the impression, and wrongly, that Simon Crole was in a state of perpetual surprise.

His eyes swerved from the tabloid sheet as the interoffice phone buzzed. He took down the receiver and spoke into it, softly. "Good morning, precious."

Etta's voice purred sweetly over the wire. "A gentleman to see you by the name of Lefty Swope."

"I don't know him. What's he want?"

"I am not clairvoyant."

"Then send him in." He hung up.

Lefty Swope swaggered through the door, his left shoulder held high, his jaw outthrust, teeth grinding on something in his mouth. One eyelid drew down more than the other as if that eye could not quite make up its mind whether to remain closed or open.

Simon Crole smiled expansively. "How are you, Lefty?"

"Aw, not so good. Quite a place you got here. Must make a lot of money?"

Crole looked at his meager furnishings as if seeing them for the first time. "No," he admitted sadly. "The stuff is ancient. I thought for a moment that the place was really better than it was."

"Aw, the hell with it," said Lefty. "I ain't trying to start an argument. I come here because they's a guy in this town I don't like. I'm in business. See? It's legit all right. But this guy don't like me, see? Nor I, him. It's mutual."

"You don't like each other, eh? That it?"

"That's only half of it. We ain't never going to like each other. I opens a little food joint. Chili beans, hamburgers, you know—all that sort of thing. Along comes this Greek and opens a place right across the street and starts to undersell me. He can afford to. He steals all his stuff. His whole family works for him . . ."

Crole raised his hand. "Let's get this straight. You don't like this Greek. Okay. What do you expect *me* to do?"

"I want you to send a couple of plug-uglies up to his joint and beat him up. Every day I want that Greek beat up until . . ."

Simon Crole sighed. "Lefty, I sympathize with you. This Greek should be beat up. But that isn't my business."

"You got detectives working for you, ain't you? Huskies that know how to handle tough guys like this Greek? Hell, I'll pay. I'll pay ten bucks every time the Greek gets knocked for a loop."

Simon Crole took papers from his pocket and rolled a flat cigarette and got out his trick lighter. It worked the first time. He smiled unbelievingly at this minor miracle. "My agency, Lefty," he said, mildly, "never undertakes a case for less than a single day's work. And the fee is a flat hundred and fifty a day."

Lefty's partially closed eye opened. "The hell you say? Why, I could get the Greek bumped off for half that amount."

"I wouldn't do that if I were you. Get you into trouble. Tell you what I will do, however. I'll give you the name and address of a man who will talk business with you and no questions asked."

From his desk pad he tore off a piece of paper and scribbled a name and address. "There you are," he said, pushing the paper across the desk. "Go and see this man. Give him ten bucks and he'll chew your Greek's ear off."

He nodded a brusk dismissal.

"Thanks. How much this gonna cost me?"

"The service is gratis. Good day."

"S'long, Mr. Crole."

After the man had left Simon Crole again picked up the tabloid. Again the buzzer. He took down the receiver.

Etta's honeyed voice said: "A lady to see you."

"Send her in."

A hard-looking blonde entered. Her lips were like two pieces of straight, red string. Above them were sullen eyes, heavily daubed with mascara. "Betty Autry is my name," she began.

Crole nodded pleasantly, but felt otherwise. Long training enabled him to recognize the type. He wouldn't get along with this woman.

"It's about my husband," continued Betty Autry. "I want a quick divorce and plenty of alimony. My husband is wealthy. But he's tight, stays away from other women, and objects to my having a good time. You know how to arrange things like this, don't you?"

Crole nodded. "Yes. I could handle this very nicely. In other words, Mrs. Autry, you want your husband framed—a sort of a modern badger game. Infidelity, divorce, then alimony. The three always seem to follow each other."

Betty Autry nodded. Her sullen eyes were on those of the private detective. "I want it so that I'll get the divorce on good grounds so that the judge . . ."

"I'm sorry," said Crole, shaking his bald head. "Framing people isn't my type of business. You'll have to try some other agency."

Fury blazed in Betty Autry's eyes. "If it's a question of money . . . ?"

"Not in the least. My reputation, Mrs. Autry, is really something I must consider. My business is legal and licensed, and I'm under bond. And since it's my business, I reserve the right to choose my cases. I'm sorry, of course, that . . ."

Something very much like an animal snarl parted the red strings that formed this selfish woman's lips. "If that's the way you feel about it, I'll find another agency. There are plenty in this city. Good day, Mister Simon Sanctimonious Crole." The hall door slammed viciously behind her.

Simon Crole got to his feet and wandered into Etta's office. "Precious," he asked his secretary, "is there something about my face or clothes that makes me look like a thug or a cheap operator?"

Etta eyed him blandly. "You're not handsome, if that's what . . ."

"It isn't what I mean at all. The clients—they're getting worse all the time. We haven't had a quality case in . . ."

The hall door opened. A Mexican in a chocolate-brown suit sidled in. He smiled apologetically at the private detective. "Am I speaking to Señor Crole?" he asked in very good English.

Simon nodded. "Come inside." He shrugged helplessly. "Now. What is it you want?"

"Your help, Señor Crole. It concerns my erring son."

"You and everybody else want my help. This seems to be my free clinic day."

"I will not trouble you very much."

"Sit down. Start talking."

"José Hernandez," said the Mexican, sitting down, "is my name." Here he took out a fat roll of money. "So that you will understand I expect to pay my debt." He smiled wistfully.

"I'm glad you expect to pay, José. All my customers today have been poor. Those that weren't poor were bad people."

"I also am poor, but not bad. You are not of the police, are you?"

"No. I am not of the police."

"That is very nice. The police I distrust. Now. My son, Manuel, is a good boy, but he does not work. Soon I shall take him into my business. But he does not wish it. He would rather loaf and regard the legs of girls who labor in the walnut packing plant. He has ideas—most of them will cause trouble."

"I think I understand, José. Your boy is good, but he's keeping the wrong kind of company, and you're afraid he'll get arrested by the police."

José nodded vigorously.

"You want me, perhaps, to put the fear of God into him so that he'll keep going straight."

Perplexity returned to José's eyes.

"Scare hell out of him," said Crole.

"That is what I desire," beamed the boy's parent.

Crole took down the Mexican's address. "I'll send one of my men out to your place tonight. You point out your son. My man will take care of the rest."

Honest José Hernandez extended his entire roll. Simon Crole looked at it longingly, then shook his head. "If it works out, José," he said, "you pay me ten dollars."

"Good. Some day I pay you ten dollars. Thank you." He smiled apologetically once more and left the office.

Simon Crole fashioned a cigarette and lit it with a match rather than face disappointment in the trick lighter. "Matt!" he called aloud.

Matt Ridley, Crole's only operator, came out of the adjoining room. His hat was on the back of his head. He looked bewildered, which he probably was, for he never thoroughly understood the motives of the man he worked for. His chief value to Simon Crole was an utter lack of fear, a zest for investigation, and an unswerving loyalty that was above any form of bribe.

Matt nodded. "I saw the roll he was holding in his hand more than I saw him. Funny colored suit. Talked good English, and likes his kids, as all Mexicans do."

"You're improving," said Crole. "Well," pushing the name and address across the desk, "you go up and see him tonight. He'll point out his kid. Just act natural and he'll think you're a flatfoot. Then flash your badge—not too close. And give him the works. Threaten to take him to jail where they work hell out of the prisoners. And anything else you can think of. But scare him—and scare him good."

"I'll give him a scare that'll freeze his insides." He rubbed his palms together. "You turned down money in that Autry woman."

"I know it," said Crole.

"I hope," said Matt, staring at the bottom drawer of Crole's desk, "that you haven't been smacked by the reform bug. You turn down a case involving thousands of dollars, and take on a poor Spig for a ten dollar fee. No business of mine, though. I could do with a snack of that Bourbon in the bottom drawer. I know it's there be . . ."

The buzzer sounded. Matt sighed and turned regretfully away. Crole took down the receiver, listened and said wearily: "Send him in, precious. My day is ruined anyway."

A man with a thin, tanned face entered, nodded and dropped into a comfortable position on the leather couch. "Ned Anderson is my name. I'm an incompetent sort of a person, so I have been told. I'm easy-going, shiftless and inclined to be tolerant about everything and everybody."

Simon Crole squinted at his caller. "That's quite a confession. Are you sober?"

"Quite. Been so since last night."

"What's on your mind?"

"First, let's get *me* straight. I'm an old friend of Esther Manning who . . ."

"Worked as a store detective," finished Crole. "She also worked for me once, then graduated into police work, social welfare, and now she has her own law office."

"She sent me here," said Anderson. "I've been away— around the world. I just got back. Yesterday. Heard some bad news regarding my estate. Everything gone. Money, stocks and bonds, and a twenty-one room house in Los Gatos canyon."

"You mean," said Crole, "that while you were away . . ."

"While I was away I was robbed by the man who was supposed to protect my estate."

"How could a man get away with anything like that? Didn't you have papers to sign? Didn't you realize . . .?"

"I signed a paper before I left giving this gentleman full power of attorney over everything I possessed."

"Oh!" Simon Crole rubbed a knuckle against his nose. "Lose much in the transaction?"

"Well over two hundred thousand, plus that twenty-one room house in Los Gatos canyon."

Crole drummed the desk top with his fingers. "That's a large sum, Mr. Anderson. We'll leave the house out of the discussion and stick to the money part."

"No," insisted Ned Anderson. "That house belonged to me and I used to like it. Still do. Want it back."

Crole shrugged. "What's the gentleman's name?"

"James Gillespie. Investment counselor, broker and all that sort of thing."

"If Gillespie is guilty of defrauding you out of your estate, Anderson, it looks to me like a case for the police and the courts. When did you discover your loss?"

"At my hotel last night I had a visitor—a girl named Virginia Laird, secretary for Gillespie. She came to me because she thought I was a sap to hand everything I owned over to Gillespie. She told me that Gillespie was losing heavily in the stock market and that a check against my personal funds for seventeen thousand dollars had, by mistake, passed through her hands. It seems Gillespie lost all his own money in Wall Street."

"What else do you know?"

"The girl left me, wouldn't let me take her home. I started to follow her for some reason I afterwards forgot. On the street outside a man posing as a police detective grabbed her and tried to sneak her away in a cab."

Crole's eyes seemed heavy with sleep. "Well?"

"I didn't like to see the girl manhandled so I got a little rough with the man who told her he was a detective. They drove away without the girl. Afterwards I took her home."

"You figure that someone was watching the girl and heard what she told you?"

Ned Anderson nodded. "Yes."

"When did you check up on your losses?"

"This morning, as soon as the bank opened. I also called the Tax Assessor's office. The house in Los Gatos canyon is no longer mine. It belongs to some gentleman in London."

"Were you wiped out entirely?"

"Three thousand dollars is all I've got left."

"And your object in coming to me, Anderson, is to get your money and property back?"

"Esther Manning said you were the best private dick in town. Said also that if anybody could get it back you could."

"My fees for this class of work are heavy, Anderson."

"The sky's the limit with me. Any part of the three thousand I've got is yours as a retaining fee. Name your figure."

"One thousand down, Anderson."

Ned Anderson took a check book from his pocket, wrote rapidly and placed the oblong of paper on the agency man's desk. Crole eyed the piece of paper meditatively without picking it up.

"About this Gillespie. I suppose you had a rather violent scene with him in his office this morning before coming here?"

"I went there for that particular purpose," said Anderson, calmly. "The door was open. But the office was deserted. No one was there. The place was somewhat upset. Even the safe door was open. It looks to me as if Mr. Gillespie had departed rather suddenly."

"Wait," said Crole. He took down the receiver and spoke to his secretary. "Dial James Gillespie's office. If anybody answers, ask for Gillespie." He hung up.

After a time Etta's voice came over the wire. "No one answers."

Simon Crole's eyebrows moved up. "She reports that no one answers."

"That's the devil of it," said Ned Anderson, moodily. "I'm not surprised at Gillespie skipping out. That's to be expected. But it's the girl I'm worried about."

"The girl?"

"Yes, Miss Laird, Gillespie's secretary. I called her home this morning. Talked with her mother. Found out that she had gone to work as usual. Whether she ever reached the office or not I couldn't find out. But somebody had been there, that's certain."

"You think, Anderson, that Miss Laird . . ."

"I'm hiring you to do the thinking, Crole. Gillespie knew that she had certain knowledge of that seventeen-thousand dollar check. Someone must have hired that man who tried to force her into the taxi last night. If Gillespie isn't back of it, then who the devil is?" Simon Crole smiled benignly. The case had its angles, and right now, they appeared sharply defined.

He had merely to locate Gillespie, apply pressure of the right sort—a threat of criminal action in courts that were not lenient with malefactors of this type of swindling—force Gillespie to disgorge, collect an additional fee, and close the case. He started to roll a cigarette when Ned Anderson's voice stopped him.

"If anything happens to that girl, Crole, if she's been kidnapped . . ."

"You mean murder?"

"Exactly!"

The benign expression fled from Simon Crole's face. "I begin to see why you've come to me. But if it's murder, Anderson, the case will partly pass out of my hands, but I'll see that your interests are protected."

"When will you start?"

"I suppose," said Crole, picking up the check and rising to his feet, "that I had better start at once. It is understood, of course, that I am the only one you have engaged to investigate your affairs."

"You're the only one."

"Let's go," said Crole, "and see if we can find the estimable James Gillespie."

At Etta's desk on the way out he stopped, endorsed the check and handed it to her. "Open an account with Mr. Ned Anderson. Credit it with this amount, and give me some money, fifty dollars from my personal account."

Smiling, he turned his big, round face on his new client. "All right, Anderson. Your affairs are about to be put in order, without, I hope, too much skullduggery."

CHAPTER IV

THE MISSING BROKER

THE DOOR OPENED EASILY.

Simon Crole stepped boldly into James Gillespie's luxurious office. Behind him tagged Ned Anderson, pale and remote.

The room in which he found himself was large, airy, and quite empty. One of the windows was open. Beside it stood a safe. That, too, was open. The open safe was the first thing Crole noticed.

"Close the door," he said quietly, "and sit down so you'll be out of my way. I'm going to snoop around while I have the chance."

"Start your snooping," yawned Anderson, dropping with a grunt into a chair near the hall door. "I wish you luck, but it looks to me like we're too late. I guess I'm licked, Crole. A fellow on the boat, a Swami, told my fortune. He said I was making my homeward journey when the stars were cockeyed. He said that certain planets—and he meant the evil ones—were up to no good as far as I was concerned. Said also that alcoholic tendencies were going to exert a tremendous . . ."

"Skip it," said Crole. "Get your mind off the Swami. I don't care what he told you. Listen to me. This case is in my hands. I know what it takes to straighten it out. A fee. Okay. You paid your fee. In a couple of days you'll be back among the moneyed class. I ain't kidding you."

"I damned well hope you're right," said Anderson. "Listen, Crole, why didn't we stop at the Rainbow Grill before coming up here? My nerves are taut as fiddle strings."

Crole regarded his client as one would a sulky child. "Forget it. Now sit back and take it easy. Don't talk to me. Don't talk to yourself. Just leave this puzzle to Simon, and everything will be jake."

Anderson's eyes became wells of sorrow. "Okay, Simon."

Simon Crole turned his attention to the room that was James Gillespie's office. He walked to the center of the room, and with feet spread wide allowed his eyes to range over floor, walls and ceiling. Then they concentrated on the furniture.

He wondered, idly, if the closing of what appeared a usual fraud case was going to be as simple as he had first thought it would be. He decided it was. He even speculated on how much of the fee he had already collected would have to be returned to client Anderson.

His lips puffed out as he walked to a desk that was obviously Gillespie's. Behind it was a mahogany chair the same as the desk. Rich, comfortable furniture. The rug beneath the chair felt as if it must be two inches thick.

Crole sighed as he bent over the mahogany desk. Boldly he opened the various drawers and pawed amongst their contents. His eyes were sharp as a ferret's. He drew back a little. What was it he looked for? What did he expect to find by snooping? It occurred to him that he was merely putting on a show to impress his client. This wasn't so good. He really should have left Anderson downstairs, or not brought him at all.

Thoughtfully he rubbed the side of his nose and peered under the desk. He lifted out a waste basket, fumbled through its contents, glanced sideways at Anderson, who was staring moodily into space, then pushed the basket back beneath the desk. He saw then, for the first time, an oblong of cardboard on the rug that hadn't been there when he first looked. Must have been hidden beneath the basket. Anyway, it was there now.

The oblong of cardboard had a piece of dirty string attached to it, and sometime in the past its corners had been cut off. It looked like a tag of some sort that might have been attached to a trunk or a key. Crole glanced at both sides of it, saw a faint trace of writing impossible to decipher, grunted and tucked it in his pocket.

From his position near the door Anderson began to hum a dolorous tune he had picked up while sojourning in Africa. It was a sad, minor lamentation that undoubtedly expressed a gnawing sorrow.

"Don't do that," admonished Crole. "It keeps me from hearing footsteps in the hall."

Anderson blinked. "I could do that much at least."

"Missed the point," said Crole. "Try again."

"I meant I could listen for footsteps if it would help you."

"Oh! All right. You keep your ears open and say when. And listen some more. If anyone comes in, you go out, see? And I'll follow soon after."

Anderson nodded. "If my eyes are closed, Simon, it doesn't mean I'm asleep. I think and listen better when they're that way."

"Just so long as you know your own habits. Well, I'm not through yet. So far everything looks right—except the open door of the safe."

He again took a stance in the center of the room, legs spread wide, hands plunged deep in the side pockets of his coat. He noticed for the first time the water cooler to the right of the safe. He took a wax-paper cup from a nearby container and pressed his thumb against a pressure faucet. Noisily he drank.

"Are you drinking water?" shuddered Anderson.

"Nope, just playing with the gadget," admitted Crole. He went over to Virginia Laird's desk. Metal mail baskets were empty. He turned back the desk top. Up popped a typewriter. Lowering the machine into its former hiding place he next opened the top right-hand drawer.

In it was a lipstick, a handkerchief, a box of odds and ends—outworn erasers, pencil stubs and a compact the size of a half dollar.

Simon Crole pursed his lips again and tipped the front end of the box upward. Underneath was a folded paper. He smoothed it open and read:

"Dear Mr. A: As you see your doubts and suspicions were purely imaginative. Whatever Mr. G's relations to you, he has, apparently, no animosity towards me. Very friendly this morning. Perhaps that check I spoke to you about was a bank mistake after all. Let's forget it. Am being sent out on an important errand. Will finish this note later . . . vl"

"Find something?" asked Anderson, rousing up.

"Excuse me," said Crole gravely. "It's for you."

Ned Anderson took the paper from Simon Crole's hand. His eyes took in the meaning of the typed words, then became jumpy as he arrived at the signature.

"Looks like everything's going to be all right, eh?"

Crole's big head wagged solemnly back and forth. "Don't forget what you told me in the office. You checked at the bank, and at the tax assessor's office. Have you forgotten?"

"Oh hell!" sighed Anderson.

"Another pill that will have to be swallowed," said Crole. "Miss Laird was here in this office—this morning. Gillespie evidently sent her out somewhere. She hasn't come back. There's that to consider as well as the fact that Gillespie himself is missing."

He turned sideways. There were footsteps in the hall. Crole sat down. Whoever it was passed down the hall to another office.

Crole got up. His eyes were on a door set flush with the left hand wall. Evidently it led to a storeroom. He fingered the knob, twisted it and shoved the door inwards, and with the same movement thrust his head and shoulders inside.

He heard, even before a meteor exploded inside his skull, the swish of the descending blackjack. Instinctively, he allowed his big body to sag and ride the blow. The blackjack caught him just above the ear, and Simon Crole's lights went out without even a flicker.

A man stepped from behind the door, plunged through the opening. The lapels of his coat were turned up around his throat, and the rim of a gray felt hat drooped low over forehead and eyes.

Anderson came surging to his feet. But he was a little slow. The blackjack thocked down hard. He staggered, groaned and fell into a curled heap.

The man with the blackjack pocketed the weapon, turned down the lapels of his coat, flung a final, despairing glance at the quiet body of the agency man, and closed the door softly behind him.

Etta's smile was a thing of serenity when Simon Crole trudged through the hall door. "It's about time you got back. Four clients since you've been gone. I had to send them to another agency." She noticed the bump and discoloration on the side of his head as he removed his hat. "You been in a taxi smash-up?"

Simon Crole sat down on a chair near his secretary. "Nope. No taxi smash-up. Just a plain, everyday blackjack. If I hadn't dropped with the blow, I'd still been out."

He took a sack of tobacco from his pocket and rolled a cigarette. Etta supplied the match and asked a question: "Anderson case?"

Crole nodded. "Ahunh."

"Starting off swell. For all I know you may get bumped off the way you go barging around. What's the matter with taking Matt with you once in a while? He knows how to take care of himself when in danger."

"I didn't know," sighed Crole, inhaling, "how close I was to danger. I was never so taken by surprise in my life."

"You're becoming senile. Listen, I heard Anderson talking before you took his case, and I say that any man that defrauds another man to the grand tune of a couple hundred thousand plus a twenty-one room house, is some dangerous man."

"Always you're right, precious. I walked into this thing with my eyes open, but I wasn't watching where I was going. However, Anderson got kicked by the same horse."

He twisted in his chair. "Matt!" he called.

Ridley came out of the office adjoining Crole's rubbing his eyes. "Sorry to wake you," said Crole, "but I guess you'll have to go to work." He looked at his watch. "There's still plenty of time before you'll have to tackle that Hernandez kid. Now listen."

Briefly he recounted what had already happened. "So," he finished, "I opened this door to see what was behind it. I found out—almost. I should have spotted that door the first thing. The safe was wide open to wind and rain. And nobody in sight. I kept wondering about that safe door, but I never connected it with the other door."

Ridley looked at the swelling on his boss's head. "Smacked you pretty. But what happened to Anderson?"

"Same thing. He was a little longer coming to his senses. I took him to his hotel, placed a bottle in his hands, said *adios,* and came back to the office."

"And what's this job you mentioned?"

"Before Anderson went down for the count, he got a look at a shield. You see this man had his hat pulled down and his coat lapels turned up around neck and chin. It showed his badge pretty."

"Cop?" asked Ridley.

"Nope. Private agency like ourselves. Anyhow, here's the dope. I want you to get into Gillespie's apartment if possible. I've got an idea this agency is working for him. I think this man that was in the storeroom was the same gent who tried to snatch Miss Laird last night."

"You figure Gillespie will be in his apartment?"

"I figure he's already skipped to another part of the city. No, he won't be there, but at the same time I want to be sure. And it's barely possible you'll run into some agency man you're familiar with. Now get going and call me back the first chance you get."

Matt Ridley looked up the address in the telephone directory, copied it in a book and went back to the room adjoining Crole's. When he emerged some minutes later he wore the uniform of the gas company's employee, and carried a satchel of tools.

"If they's one thing I like," said Matt, setting his tools on the desk and lighting a cigarette, "it's being a gas inspector. It always goes over big."

"On your way," said Etta. "I've seen you in that coat before, and heard that same line of chatter."

"Chatter," scoffed Matt. "That's all you do. Your trap goes like a squirrel's." He grinned and winked. "When I come back I'll bring you a bag of nuts."

"A drink," sighed Crole, rising to his feet. "That's what I need. A good shot of Bourbon and I'll be okay again." Through half-closed eyes he looked at his operator. "And that don't include you. Close the door softly and don't forget to ring me back."

In less than an hour the phone rang. Etta relayed the call to Crole. He took down the receiver. Matt's voice crackled over the wire and into the receiver.

"I'm inside, boss. Been here above fifteen minutes. Got the gas range almost entirely apart in case anyone shows up. The apartment is empty as far as Gillespie is concerned. But his clothes are all here. No bags packed, and no orders to discontinue the utility services. So I guess he ain't gone very far."

"Listen, Matt. If he had made arrangements to leave the city, he wouldn't advertise the fact by notifying the utility companies. Hang around a while longer and keep your eyes opened for anyone who looks like a private dick."

"Okay. I'm doing a swell job on this gas range. I didn't know I was so good. Bye."

"Bye," said Crole, snapping the receiver in place.

Attorney George Baron looked up from the air-line maps he had been studying. In front of his desk stood two men. One was pale, with a face like a boy. The face was void of expression. This man stood leaning back on his heels, his hands thrust deep in the side pockets of his coat. He was known as Ghost Mokund—and he looked ghostly.

Beside him stood another man, broad of girth, round, ham-like face, thick lips and a big mouth. They both wore caps, were well dressed, and slightly covered with dust. This second man had various names. But at this particular moment and in this town he called himself Selingo. He specialized in mayhem in its various horrible aspects, and was inordinately proud of his reputation.

"Well," said Selingo, "this guy Smith has been given the works. I don't like to brag, pal, but when Ghost and me team up on a guy, he ain't got no more chance of keeping out of hell than the Devil himself."

"Humm!" grunted Mokund.

"I see," approved Baron. "And you . . . you saw to it that the car burst into flames . . ."

"Did we," chortled Selingo. "I'll tell the cockeyed world. Am I right, Ghost?"

"Humm!" grunted Mokund.

"He ain't very talkative," explained Selingo, his mouth twisting in a Gargantuan leer, "but he can do things with a car, a rod and chemicals. I've seen him go half way up a telephone pole without cracking a fender."

From a desk drawer George Baron removed a package of currency. "Five thousand," he said. "Right?"

"I don't know," said Selingo, "and won't know till I finish counting." He spat on his hands and started to count the bills in the package. "Five grand is right," he nodded. "Damn lucky thing for you, mister, that it was right. I hates chiselers."

Mokund grunted a third time.

"He does, too," added Selingo, pocketing the money. "Well, I guess we'll push on, Mr. Baron. They's a lot of cops in this town—the kind that look like they take nobody's lip."

"I'm glad you noticed that, Selingo. Our cops *are* dangerous, fast on the draw and crack shots. That's why I imported you men from the east. Killers don't last long around here. It might be wise if you both got out of the state—at once."

"Cops don't bother me," said Selingo. "I know how to get along with them. Ran into a barrier at the border. Nothing to it. Slipped a sergeant a twenty and he almost kissed me."

Baron shrugged. "That sergeant wasn't looking for you. He was only stationed there to keep out the indigent."

"What's indigent?"

George Baron smiled suavely. "The poor."

"Geez!" spat Selingo. "Don't it beat hell how the poor are always the goats."

Ghost Mokund waxed eloquent. "You said it, Selingo."

On the street outside Selingo turned to his companion in crime. "Ghost," he said, gravely, "that guy what just turned over five grand to us is not a big shot. He's wise all right— all mouthpieces are. But he seemed in a hell of a yank to get us out of the state."

Ghost Mokund lit a cigarette and stared gloomily towards the parking place where he had left the red, low-slung car.

Selingo had expected no answer so he went on. "I figure it like this, Ghost. The cops in this town ain't got our number—yet. Our car ain't hot, neither is our money. I figure we ought to look around while we're here. Anyways I want to read in the papers about that Smith guy. Whadda yuh say. Shall we blow, or stick around."

Ghost Mokund still stared straight ahead. "Humm!" he grunted.

"Okay," beamed Selingo. "We'll stick around."

The snap decision of these two tough gentlemen was later to cause a dark shadow to fall over George Baron. But that suave and shrewd attorney had already thrust these men from his mind. Other and more important pawns were about to be moved on the checkerboard of crime on which he had constituted himself a prime mover.

His eyes, level and keen, were on a man standing before his desk, studying him, weighing him, wondering just how far he could trust him. Coughlin stood there, his hat on the side of his head, his lips twisted into a leer.

"It's all off, Baron. It isn't that I have any scruples against handling your dirty work. I lost all decency and honor years ago. The system took it all out of me."

"You mean," said Baron, quietly, "that you're quitting me? I don't like it, Coughlin. Not in the least."

"Sure, I'm quitting. I know when I'm licked."

"All right. Suppose you start at the beginning."

"At Gillespie's office this afternoon. I went there . . ."

"Yes, I know why you went there."

"Two men came in. I was forced to hide in a closet. While I was in there I listened to their voices. One was Ned Anderson, the same guy that took a poke at me while I was getting the girl in the cab. The other was . . ."

Baron lighted a panatela. He seemed not to be listening.

"Simon Crole," finished Coughlin.

The eyebrows of the attorney arched interrogatively. "Simon Crole did you say? And who might Crole be?"

Coughlin laughed sourly. "Just another private dick like myself."

"What's so unusual in that situation?"

"The unusual part in that situation, I keep telling you, is that the guy who was with Anderson was Simon Crole, the smartest and the most tricky private detective in town. Believe me I'd rather have the whole city's police department after me than this one man."

"What's the matter, losing your nerve?" queried Baron.

"You don't know Crole. I do."

"So what am I supposed to do?"

"If you'll take my advice, you'll pack your bags and get out of town. Crole is that kind of a guy. If Anderson is his client, somebody will have to give Anderson his money back. As simple as that. I ain't foolin'. Lucky thing for me I had a blackjack in my pocket. Neither of them got a good look at my face, but I sweat plenty before I got into the clear."

Baron savored the aroma of his cigar. He did not seem alarmed. Nor did his voice lose any of its cultured accent.

"On the whole, Coughlin, you've been helpful. I dislike to see you leave us at this particular time. You haven't by any chance seen Gillespie today?"

Coughlin shook his head. "He wasn't in his office, if that's what you mean."

"He's gone on a short trip, Coughlin. He was to be back late this afternoon. You know I am a trifle worried. He was always punctual with appointments. About this fellow Crole. Perhaps I had better go and see him myself. If he's as good as you say he is, it might just be possible that I can arrange with him to leave the state. Think it will work out?"

"No," said Coughlin. "It won't work out."

"Why?"

Coughlin's face reddened as rage suffused it. "Why? By God, I'll tell you why. He can't be bribed. Whatever faults he has, and they're plenty, he sticks with his clients through hell and high water. Hell, that's what's the matter with guys like me and others. We try to hog everything. Take money from both sides. Work both ends against the middle, and all for a few lousy dollars."

He paused, and his eyes became sad. "Listen, Baron. This guy isn't any saint. He's a Devil with horns, a tail and . . ."

"Nonsense."

"That's because you don't know him, Baron," snapped Coughlin. "I'll send in my bill covering the work I did for you and Gillespie. You can send me a check . . ."

"One moment, Coughlin. Has it occurred to you that I might not want you to leave me, that you know more than you should regarding certain things?"

"I know plenty, but I'm willing to forget."

"It isn't as easy as that, Coughlin. If an attempted kidnapping charge should be brought against you, the result might be serious—for you."

"You wouldn't dare. It would incriminate you and Gillespie."

"Not necessarily. Our word is as good as yours. And don't forget that Miss Laird's and Ned Anderson's testimony could be used against you. No doubt, Coughlin, you spoke too quickly without giving your words much thought." Baron's voice was slightly mocking, yet it carried a subtle threat.

Coughlin squirmed uneasily. "I still don't like having Crole for an enemy."

"Neither do I," shrugged Baron, "from what you have told me. But has it not yet dawned on you that even Crole might be removed?"

"No."

"Come back later. We'll talk over the details then."

"All right. I'll come back. But it had better be a damned good and absolutely fool-proof plan, or there'll be a kick-back."

He tilted his hat far over his eyes, squared his shoulders and marched out of attorney Baron's office.

For some minutes Baron puffed his cigar as he thought things over. Then shrugged and started to look through the telephone directory. Snapping the book shut, he got up, went into a washroom, washed his hands, combed his hair and fitted a fawn-colored felt hat to his head. These preparations attended to, he left his office and was taxied to an office building not far from his own.

He found the name he looked for listed on a wall directory, took the elevator to the sixth floor, got out, and walked up the stairs to the seventh. The hall was quiet. Stepping lightly, he moved down the hall till he came to a door labeled: SIMON CROLE, SPECIAL INVESTIGATOR.

"Every man," thought George Baron, "is a potential criminal. I have never yet seen one who didn't have his price— especially private detectives."

So thinking, he extended a manicured hand towards the door knob.

CHAPTER V

A TRIP TO THE MORGUE

MATT RIDLEY DIDN'T GET BACK to the agency office until after six o'clock. Etta had gone home. Simon Crole sat behind his scarred desk smoking a flat cigarette, his thoughts loose and disjointed.

He looked up hopefully as Matt came in, dropped the bag of tools on the floor and peeled off the gas company uniform. Dressed in street clothes once more he came over to Simon's desk.

Crole said: "Well?"

Matt shrugged. "Nobody came into the apartment but the housekeeper. She hollered to beat hell when she saw I had the stove apart. After I got her cooled she began to talk. Gillespie lives there alone except for this woman who comes in and cooks his meals. He has few friends and keeps pretty much to himself. He drives a Buick coupe and keeps it in a garage back of the apartment building. It wasn't there when I left nor was it on the street. So he's probably in it now—somewhere."

Crole regarded the cigarette already beginning to get hot against his fingers. "See anything of any other agency men around?"

"Nope."

Simon Crole grunted. "We're getting nowheres fast, Matt."

"That ain't unusual. Maybe we're headed the wrong direction. Maybe Gillespie took his secretary for a little jaunt to the beach. As far as I can see there wasn't any signs around the apartment that he was running away."

"But he wasn't there."

"Yeah, I know that. But listen, boss. You say we're getting nowheres fast. Where are we headed for in the first place?"

"A showdown with Gillespie. A talk with his secretary. Looks easy—and should be. But both are missing, the office is open and empty including the safe. Seems queer, Matt, that a man planning to run away would leave everything loose like that."

"Go on," said Matt. "You're doing swell."

"Another thing. Suppose Gillespie suddenly made up his mind to leave for parts unknown. He wouldn't bother much about the stuff he left behind. Suppose he already had all the available funds of his business converted into cash. Suppose he had it figured out that he'd have to do one of two things. Either meet Anderson face to face and explain what he had done and try to straighten up the mess, or gather everything of value together and fade from the picture."

"Figuring it that way, it looks like he was fading."

"On his way out of the city, say," continued Crole, "Gillespie suddenly recollects something he left in his safe. It's important. He has to have it. So he sends someone to his office to get it. About that time I arrive with Anderson. Then this man hides in the storeroom. He hears us talk. He hears Anderson call me by name. He knows me. And he doesn't like it. Then he smacks me down and . . ."

"And fades the same as Gillespie," finished Matt. "It's a good idea, boss, but it doesn't take care of the jane secretary."

"That's the part that's giving me a headache. I *know* she was in that office sometime during early morning. I also know that she was sent away on an important errand. So it would seem that she was not with Gillespie—but with somebody else."

Matt's eyes bulged. "You figure a snatch?"

Simon Crole shrugged. "It's too early yet to figure anything. Maybe tomorrow, maybe next week. It all depends. If the girl's been snatched, Anderson will sure as hell go to the police. And I won't be able to stop him. And the Federals will step in. Nice prospect. Everything gummed up. No fee. Nothing. Get the hell out of here. Go on home. Scram!"

Matt said: "Let's have a drink."

Simon took out his private Bourbon and two glasses. He poured one of them full, then emptied half of it in the second glass. Matt regarded his drink with an appraising eye, engulfed the glass in a big fist and downed the golden fluid.

"Give you credit, boss. You know how to pick good stuff." He set the glass down and wiped moist lips with the back of his hand. "I'm off to grab myself some supper, then I'll amble out to Spigtown and put on the heavy act with young Hernandez. The ten bucks you get from Hernandez will just about cover expenses."

"That's all I figured on," said Crole, morosely.

Matt waved jauntily and left the office.

A silence settled over the building, over Simon Crole's office. No longer was there constant clangor from the doors of the elevator cages. Crole got up and went to a window, flung it open and stared down into the street. Supper crowds. Men and women going home after a day's work. Old men newsboys shouting unintelligible jargon.

He went back to his desk, had a second drink and rolled a cigarette, then went out to Etta's desk, sat down and called Gillespie's apartment. No answer. He tried the office. Same result.

He sat for a moment trying to think. He had the feeling that somewhere along the line he had erred. He checked back. No go. There was really no point from which he could get started with Gillespie missing from the picture.

In the meantime he'd have to wait. If the man was running away to escape the consequences of his embezzling practices, well, there was nothing that he, Simon Crole, could do about it but wait until the fact was proven. As it was now his hands were tied. He could only wait . . .

His eyes abruptly slitted as they arched up from the desk top to the door leading to the hall. He had heard no sound that he was aware of, but he sensed an alien presence the other side of the door.

His body stiffened as the knob clicked, turned.

Slowly, almost imperceptibly the door swung inward. A man stood framed in the opening—a man with an aura of respectable urbanity, high cheek bones, wide-spaced eyes, and a trim gray mustache. A man faultlessly dressed, sure of himself.

Crole let out his breath with an audible sigh. Somewhere inside his brain a little bell began to ring. He had heard that bell once, long ago, a split second before a sub-machine gun had blasted the spot where he stood in a gang-infested hotel room. He had heard it later, in a gilded roadhouse just in time to avoid the shimmering steel of a thrown knife.

He heard the bell now, faint and disturbing. His mind went on guard. He placed both hands on the desk, hunched forward on the chair. And his lips were twisted in their surprised smile.

"How do you do," said the suave individual. "Mr. Simon Crole?"

Simon nodded. "Am I supposed to know you—an appointment or something?"

"My name is George Baron, business, attorney at law. You were recommended to me as being the ablest private detective in town. I need your services. I'll pay you well."

"That's fine," beamed Crole. "What is it you want?" George Baron took a cigar from his breast pocket, bit off the end, lighted it and calmly surveyed the meagre furnishings of the office in which he found himself.

"There's a man in New York I want you to find—an important witness for one of my clients. Someone paid him to run out on me. I want him located and brought back. Can you handle this quietly for me?"

"Why not?"

"Personally?"

"No. Right now I have another client who has a prior claim on my agency. But I can send a good operator, or I can arrange to find your witness through an old associate of mine who runs an agency in New York."

"That's not what I want, Crole. I want you, personally, to leave this city, go to New York and take care of this business without any outside help."

"That's asking too much, Mr. Baron. Sorry."

"I can guarantee you ten thousand dollars, Crole."

Simon Crole smiled ruefully. "That's a large lump of money for the work of finding a witness. And no one likes to collect fees better than I do. Still, I must refuse unless you let me handle it through someone else."

"Fifteen thousand, Crole."

"No."

"Twenty."

Simon Crole rubbed the heel of a thumb along the side of his nose. "I didn't think there was that much money in town, Baron—and mine for the asking. Why don't you go to some other agency? Or why didn't you come to me sooner?"

He stopped rubbing his nose, took out a sack of tobacco and deftly rolled a cigarette. He speculated as to why Mr. Baron had sought him out. Evidently for a reason—a good and sufficient one to warrant a fee of twenty thousand. Was the witness that important, or was it important that he, Simon Crole, leave town. The echo of that tiny bell was still in the brain of the private detective. He became unduly loquacious.

"To be perfectly frank, Baron, your proposition has possibilities that make me kind of ill because I can't take advantage of it. But right now I'm working on what appears to be an embezzlement case. A man named Ned Anderson has retained me to investigate the affairs of another man named James Gillespie."

"Gillespie?" George Baron's eyes showed a mild interest. "That's somewhat of a coincidence, I'd say. Why, Gillespie and I have been friends for years. In fact I'm his attorney."

Simon Crole smiled. His loquaciousness had brought startling results. It connected the two men. "It is somewhat of a coincidence, Baron. You wouldn't, by any chance, know where Gillespie is at the present moment? It's important that I see him. If I can find him and talk with him, it's likely that

I can close Anderson's case and take on yours. That's the way things stand."

George Baron fingered his gray mustache. "Ummm! I'm sorry to hear that Jim is in trouble—even a suspicion of trouble. Not that I for a single moment doubt the outcome. Embezzlement isn't his line. I think, Crole, that your client Anderson has—well, shall we say been drinking too much."

"You might call it that," mused Crole. "But if I can get James Gillespie and Anderson together, the situation can be discussed and a settlement arranged. That'll let me out. But Gillespie doesn't seem to be around. Which makes it difficult."

George Baron rose to his feet. "I'll think it over, Crole. In the meantime you can continue," he coughed lightly, "to look for Gillespie. I presume I'll hear from you when that time comes?"

"You'll hear from me," nodded Crole, also rising. "As a matter of fact I think we'll see a great deal of each other."

"Shouldn't wonder," shrugged Baron. "Good night."

Crole held open the door. "Good night."

A moment after he heard the elevator cage stop outside, Simon Crole again opened the door and looked down the corridor. The hall was empty. He clicked on the night latch and shut the door. Leaving the front office he went to his own, poured himself a drink, smacked his lips and exhaled a long, gusty sigh.

He reached for the phone and called a number, asked for Anderson, got him, and said: "Sober?"

"Cold. Why? This Crole?"

"Yes. Listen. What do you know about George Baron?"

Anderson's bored yawn came over the wire. "Sorry. Can't help."

"Heard from Miss Laird?"

"I'm going out to her house this evening. Expect to find her all right. If I can't, I'm calling in someone from the Federal office."

"Listen again, Anderson. I've just been offered twenty thousand dollars to leave town on a different case."

"Get my money back, Simon," drawled Anderson, "and I'll double the ante."

"I didn't tell you this to raise any ante."

"That's all right, too. I want you on my side—all the way. And I'll see that you don't lose. Who was . . ."

"A secret for the present. Remember, I'm leaving it to you to check up on the girl. Lay off the Federals. Leave everything to Simon. Clear?"

"Where can I get hold of you?"

"Either here or at my apartment. Get moving now and for God's sake stay sober. Bye." He hung up. Waited a few minutes, then called the switchboard operator in his apartment house.

"Darling," he called. "Simon. If a call comes for me and I'm not there, get whatever you can out of the person at the other end of the line. It might help you to know that I expect a call from a man named Anderson. Handle it right and there's a brand new five dollar bill waiting for you. Bye."

He left his desk and sauntered over to the window. Dusk was shutting down fast, and the street lights were on. Fog was sweeping in from the Pacific, obscuring the graying sky. He went back to his desk again. He stumbled over a chair and swore softly.

Uneasiness kept him from sitting down. He wondered why George Baron had offered such a huge sum. A few hundred dollars plus train tickets would cover everything in locating a missing witness. Clearly there was a connection. Were Baron and Gillespie linked with the man who had struck him down?

It was possible. But there was no way to prove it—yet. He rubbed the aching lump on his head. The man who had hidden in the storeroom must have heard them talk. And knew who was talking. They hadn't lowered their voices. And he had been in the storeroom listening. "Ummm!" he grunted, struck by an obscure hunch. "Something has happened to Gillespie. He isn't coming back."

Again he picked up the phone, called a number. "Hello. *Ledger* office? Give me the city editor." A pause. "Hello,

Farrel? Guess who? Wrong. I'm the guy who sent you a bottle of choice Scotch last Christmas. You don't remember receiving any? You news-hawks are like that. Yeah, it's Simon Crole. No, I haven't been arrested. I'm in my office."

He tucked the phone closer to his chest. "No, I got nothing to offer you now. Later maybe. What I want—let me finish. What I want to know is this. Has there been any auto accident within the last six hours? A hundred? Tck! Tck! Listen, Farrel. A blue Buick coupe. Man named Gillespie . . . oh hell! Where? When? Oh, I see. Thanks! Bye."

He slammed the receiver to the hook, groaned, found his hat, clapped it on and went stumbling out the hall door and into the first down elevator.

On the corner he bought the *Ledger* and took it with him into a coffee shop. The thing he looked for was there in a modest set-up. Had he not been aware that it was there he might have missed it entirely. His mouth twitched as he read:

COUPE IN DEATH PLUNGE

Death claimed another careless driver when James Gillespie, well known security broker, drove his machine through the guard rail at one of the switchbacks on the treacherous Iron Mountain grade early this afternoon. Fire destroyed the body past recognition, but the driver's identity was disclosed by keys, a watch and the license plates. The body was removed temporarily to the city morgue for further examination.

Simon Crole laid the paper down. Food was placed before him. He eyed it biliously. Gillespie dead. Accident or suicide? What did it matter. The two hundred thousand dollars, Crole knew, would not be in the wrecked machine. It would be hidden safely away, of that he was certain. But it would not be where either he or Anderson could touch it. He might as well forget all about it. Whatever Gillespie left behind would have to pass through the hands of an executor or some legal body. So the case was closed. And that was that.

He got up slowly, aware for the first time in many days of his big body. A promising case. A swell fee, and Gillespie, drunk, sober or plain crazy, had crashed his car off a mountain grade.

He looked at his watch, promptly forgot what he saw and shoved it back into his pocket. Abruptly he lunged out of the restaurant. A taxi took him to police headquarters. He went directly to the office of Police Captain Jorgens, a dark-faced, bitter man who chewed cigars, scowled and fought crime in all its big time sordidness. A heavy-jowled, suspicious law enforcer, honest, capable, but occasionally ham-strung with the red tape of officialdom.

The black bristles of his mustache seemed to stand out straight as his still blacker eyes focused on the round face of the private detective. He had a ponderous respect for Simon Crole's ability. Crole had solved a score of the city's big crimes, and placed the glory of the arrest and clean-up in the police captain's hands. Always the private detective had kept his own connection with these cases deep in the background, asking for no public recognition, receiving none.

Captain Jorgens would have liked to have caught Simon Crole red-handed in criminal connivance merely for his own bitter satisfaction. He would have relished nothing better than to be able to say: "Simon, your foot slipped this time. Now try and talk yourself out of it."

Small wonder that Jorgens should have his spells of occasional bitterness. He genuinely liked Simon Crole, but he hated to admit it either personally to Simon's face, or behind the private detective's back.

His eyes were moody now as they focused on the scarred lips that made Simon Crole look surprised when Jorgens knew he was not. "Hello," he said gruffly. "What's on *your* mind?"

"You don't look happy, Jorgens," said Crole. "Maybe you grin and laugh out loud when I'm not around. But the minute I appear on the scene you turn loose all your bad nature on me. But that's okay. I know you, and you know me. Now be a good shipmate and tell me I have your permission to visit the morgue and—wait a second. I also want to have a look at that blue Buick coupe that crashed through the guard rail on the Iron Mountain road this afternoon."

Captain Jorgens shrugged heavily. "What's your interest, Simon?"

"Just my curious nature getting the best of me." Captain Jorgens drummed the desk top with nervous fingers. "I don't like ambulance chasers. Can't a man have an accident without cheap lawyers and private dicks wanting to know . . ."

"Somebody else have the same idea?" asked Crole, innocently.

"No," sighed Jorgens. "That was merely a loose observation. You're the only one."

Crole rubbed his hands. "That's fine. I like to be alone. Can work better. Where's the car?"

"Where do you suppose? At the bottom of the mountain."

"Okay, Captain. I'll take a run out there tonight, and I'll look at what's left of Gillespie. Mind calling the morgue attendant and telling him I'm on my way to view the cadaver?"

"Wait a second, Crole. Have you any reason to suspect . . ."

"Nothing's ever as it seems in this world, Captain. That's what makes it so interesting, and profitable, for private detectives and other individuals."

"Nuts! An accident, I tell you. Hundreds of them every day."

"Ah!" sighed Crole. "You ought to become better acquainted with Conan Doyle. I'll amble along now. Be seeing you."

He left the captain's office and went downstairs to the morgue. The air in the long room was cold, damp and impregnated with an odor peculiar to all repositories of the dead.

The attendant in charge guided him to a slab where a body lay covered with a sheet. "I guess this is the guy you want to see. I'm warning you though that he's not a pleasant sight. Cooked just enough to be messy." Simon Crole allowed his eyes to range over the remains of James Gillespie. The hair had been burned entirely from the skull. Arms and legs were blackened. There were marks of a surgeon's scalpel on the abdomen wall.

"Autopsy," explained the attendant. "He wasn't drunk. Just in too much of a yank to get around those hair-pin turns."

Crole nodded. "Yeah. Some of them are pretty sharp. Well, I've got an eyeful. Too bad."

"Ain't it. But I guess he had plenty of insurance for his family, though. That's a point in his favor."

"Insurance?" Crole took a roll of bills from his pocket and peeled off a ten spot.

The attendant looked at the money, then at Simon Crole. "Yeah," he said, "insurance. These men came in with a flock of reporters. One of them represented the Oregon Mutual company. Didn't say who would collect, but I guess it would be plenty. The other company sent two men. They wore caps but had on new suits. Only one of them talked. The other one just grunted."

Crole smiled pleasantly. "What did these two men look like?"

"Oh, I don't know exactly. The one who grunted had a funny face—like a boy's. Smooth. No wrinkles. But he wasn't a boy. The other had a face like yours—kinda round. His lips were thicker than yours and he had a big mouth."

"You didn't hear them call each other by name, did you?"

"Nope. They said they represented the—what the hell was that company. A New York firm, the Guardian Life."

"And Gillespie was insured in both companies?"

"That's what the first man said and also those two men who came in together."

"I see," said Crole. "Lucky thing for the survivors. Well, thanks. Here, take this." He extended the bill. "Someday I might want a favor."

The attendant grinned as he pocketed the money. "Very few favors I can do for people, Mr. Crole, except show them the stiffs."

An enigmatic smile twisted Crole's face. "Yeah? You'd be surprised. By the way, when were these insurance men here?"

"I don't remember exactly—around four o'clock."

"Does Captain Jorgens know they were here?"

"I dunno. Not from anything I said. Lots of people come down here for purposes of identification. Can't keep track of all that come. Why?"

"No reason at all," shrugged Crole. "Just wondered is all."

He left the unpleasant walls of the morgue and went out onto the night street, rolled a cigarette, lit it and searched for a cab. He found one and climbed in.

"Right under Jorgens' nose," he mused, settling back against the leather cushions, "and he missed it. Insurance. Hmmmm! Two men—one with the face like a boy. He doesn't talk, merely grunts. There is something wrong with the lay-out. It isn't like insurance claim adjusters. Those adjusters can talk, and do."

He frowned into the night rushing past the taxi windows. "There's something screwy about this accident. It comes at the exact wrong time. I think, Mr. James Gillespie, those policies of yours will be worth investigating."

The cab came to a stop. Simon Crole got out. When he reached his office building, the last elevator had stopped running. Grunting his displeasure, the big agency man puffed up seven flights of stairs.

CHAPTER VI

MURDER CLUES

LIGHT GLEAMED THROUGH the frosted glass door panel when Crole reached his office. He went in. Matt was there, sitting at Etta's desk, reading the *Ledger*.

"I was on my way home when I came across this." He shoved the newspaper across the desk. "Too bad, boss."

"I read it," said Crole. "As a matter of fact I had a hunch that something might have happened to Gillespie, so I called up city editor Farrel. After reading the bad news I went down to the morgue."

"What happens next?"

"Got your car?"

"It's down in the parking lot."

"We're going for a ride. The Iron Mountain grade. Gillespie's car is still at the bottom of the gorge it plunged into. We're going to give it the once over."

Ridley said without getting up: "What'll it get you?"

"I don't know. Something. Always there's something, Matt."

"Hell, it was an accident. Tough on Gillespie. Tough on client Anderson. And tough on our office. I can see with half an eye that the case has blown up. We're out, boss, in case you don't know it."

Crole went to his desk and got out a flashlight. "I dislike to climb around mountains at night, but I guess I'll have to do it."

"Wait a minute," protested Matt. "You saw the body didn't you? It was identified, wasn't it? Okay. Then what's to be gained by scrambling down a mountain to look at a wreck?"

"Believe me, Matt, I'm not any happier about this than you are."

"You wouldn't lie to me?"

"I haven't eaten since this morning. That news item took away my appetite early this evening. I've had, maybe, four drinks all day. I had what looked like a profitable case dropped in my lap. On top of that I was smacked over the head and the man I'm looking for goes and gets himself killed. I insist I'm not happy, but that don't excuse me from this excursion to Iron Mountain."

"I'll drive you wherever you want to go," said Matt, shuffling to his feet. "And I'll slip and scramble down any mountain you can name. But I'll be damned if I can make myself understand why all this is necessary."

"Just take Simon's word for it, Matt. We're going places, me and you. Push out the lights and don't argue any more. Anderson's case isn't closed—yet. It's still wide open."

"Let's go," said Matt, resignedly. "I guess I must have spoken out of turn."

The wreckage of the Buick coupe was thorough and complete. It lay on its side, its body crushed, raked with deep scratches, and blackened inside. Crole took one look at the interior, shrugged, then began to circle it slowly.

He looked beneath it, under the hood. Flashed his light inside beneath the instrument panel, then over the charred cushions. He noticed then that in one part of the seat cushion there was a burn considerably deeper than the surrounding area.

Leaning inside he sniffed. A fire extinguisher had evidently been used by someone to quench the flames for the odor of chemicals was strongly mixed with charred cloth. He stuck his fingers into the hole and promptly cut one on a piece of broken glass. Swearing softly he withdrew his hand, the glass with it.

"Incendiary bomb," he called to Matt. "It was thrown into the car. Hmmmm!" He went around to the back, unscrewed the gas tank cap and sniffed again. "Tank a quarter full at least. So it wasn't a gas explosion that caused the fire. The car was on fire when it went through the guard rail."

Matt Ridley stood with his hands in his pockets, doing nothing. "Boss, you're making these things up." Crole screwed the cap back on the tank. "The case becomes more involved each minute. What first appeared as an accident now looks like a deliberately planned murder!"

It was Matt's turn to swear softly. He did and at some length. Finally he stopped and said: "Gillespie bumped off? Geez, boss, that's a long shot. Who's to gain by his death?"

"That's what we've got to find out. I've already got a lead. In the morning we'll check it. Meanwhile, it looks like I'll have to have a heart to heart talk with Captain Jorgens."

"You seen all you want to see?"

"I've found out plenty—here. Let's go back to the road."

Once they reached the highway Simon Crole didn't immediately get into the car. Instead he walked uphill till he came to a turnout. The ground dirt was crisscrossed with the marks of tires. He examined them for a moment, then returned to the break in the guard rail.

Wheel marks showed that the Buick was going uphill and on the wrong side of the road. Just before the break in the rail, there were skid marks in the macadam that indicated either a sharp twisting of the steering wheel, or sudden pressure from the right against the Buick's fender and front wheels.

There were other marks of tires biting into the soft macadam at the left of the road. Crole took one look at the design. The tires of the second car left a series of oblique lines.

Matt following close behind, peered also at the tire tracks.

"What make?" asked Crole.

"Generals," said Matt. "A high-priced tire on a high-priced car. That's only a guess about the car though."

"Look at those tracks and skid marks carefully, Matt, and tell me what you see. I want to see if it conforms with my own guess."

Ridley pointed at the skid marks. "Those were made by the Buick, this afternoon when the sun had softened the macadam. The car was moving uphill, probably in the center of the road. Another car comes up behind, squeezes in between the Buick and the right shoulder of the road, then swerves to the left. The Buick don't give ground, so this other car nails it about here." He indicated a left-angle skid mark.

"Keep going," said Crole.

"When the cars came together the Buick was forced over the edge through the rail, and the other car just barely swerved back to the road, judging by the tracks farther up the hill."

"Excellent," beamed Crole. "Let's go home."

The girl at the switchboard at Crole's apartment house turned to the private detective as he came through the door.

"A Mr. Anderson has been calling for the past two hours."

"Leave any message?"

"You're to call him at his hotel."

"All right. Put through the call. I'll take it in the apartment." He sighed, reached in his pocket, removed therefrom a five-dollar bill. "This isn't a tip, dear. I'm giving it to you out of a generous heart. But don't overlook any calls for me during the next couple of days."

Upstairs in his apartment he took off his coat, flung his hat on the living room table and poured himself a drink from a partially filled decanter. But before he could lift the glass to his lips the phone rang sharply. He reached for the instrument, fumbled the glass and it splintered against the floor.

"Hello," he said, gazing soberly at the broken glass on the floor. "Anderson? Your voice sounds kind of thick. What's the trouble? Oh, the girl. You couldn't find her. Well, don't worry. She'll turn up. I know how you feel. But remember, she was a stranger to you. You don't know her friends or habits. And she may have been sent out of town. Better take a drink and go to sleep."

He hung up and with his foot pushed the broken glass under the table. Thoughtfully he filled a second glass and drained it. Content for the moment he searched for tobacco and papers. His fingers encountered a small oblong of cardboard. He regarded it dully for a moment before realization dawned as to where he had found it.

There were marks on the card, but they were so faint as to be almost invisible. He'd have to examine it with his microscope at the office. He tucked it back in his pocket, paced up and down the room a couple of times, then picked up the telephone, spoke a number and was connected with Police Headquarters.

"Captain Jorgens? Simon Crole. Listen. I'm giving you a hot tip. But understand, Captain, that my name isn't to figure in what might develop. Swell, now listen.

"The man who was identified as James Gillespie was not an accident victim. He was murdered! Get it? Bye."

Officialdom taken care of, Simon Crole felt he could relax. He went out to a kitchenette in the back of his apartment and began to rummage in an electric refrigerator.

On a small table he set two bottles of beer, a chunk of salami, crackers, cheese and an unopened bottle of gherkin pickles. He flanked these solids with condiments, ketchup, mustard, hauled up a chair and sat down with a contented sigh.

The phone rang—a discordant jangling.

Crole pushed back his chair and went into the living room. He took the receiver down. "Yeah," he said.

Matt Ridley's voice came over the wire. "I forgot to tell you about young Hernandez. I scared him all right. Scared the hell out of him. He thought I was gonna take him to jail. Geez, was I good. I took him to his father. The old man said if I'd give the kid another chance, he'd get him a job in the walnut packing house. So young Hernandez agreed, and so did I."

Crole said crossly. "Gwan to bed. I'm trying to eat."

He set the phone down, yawned, stretched and went back to the little table in the kitchenette. But the scream of a siren down the street halted him before he reached it.

Pivoting, he moved determinedly through the apartment to a front window, pulled the shade aside and looked down at the curb. A police car was sliding to a stop out front.

"Oh hell!" he muttered. "I should have known better than to merely suggest something to Jorgens."

The big fist of the Police Captain was banging on the door panel. Simon Crole left the window and opened the door. "Well, well," he said. "I heard the siren ten blocks away. Figured there must at least be a bank robbery in the offing, or a massacre."

"Skip it, Simon," growled Jorgens, kicking the door shut with his heel. "Sour humor like yours is wasted on me. What's this business about murder? Damn it, you could have given me some idea instead of hanging up."

"Did I say something about murder?"

"You most certainly did."

Crole shrugged resignedly. "Have a drink, Captain?"

"A small one. What's this under the table?"

"A liquor glass I dropped. Got excited answering the telephone."

"You're getting old, Simon." Jorgens sipped his drink, his dark, bitter eyes on the agency man. "What about this murder?"

"I drove out to Iron Mountain. Climbed down the ravine where I found the wreck. Quite a blaze inside that car. It struck me as not quite right."

"We're talking about murder."

"I'm getting around to it in my own clumsy fashion. That fire inside the coupe didn't look right. I examined the car, gas tank, vacuum tank, carburetor and feed pipes. All okey. Not a pipe torn loose, nor a broken connection. Electric wires okey, and no sign of a short circuit."

"But the car burned. You can't get away from that."

"It burned, Captain, for the simple reason that someone— the actual murderer—threw an incendiary bomb into it. I found a deep hole in the seat cushion, and some glass that held the inflammable liquid, whatever it was."

"You figure . . ."

"I don't figure at all. I examined the highway and found ample evidence that proved the Buick was forced from the road. The marks were plain. This was no accident. It was a deliberately planned murder."

"And the motive?"

"That's your job, not mine. I'm pointing out obvious things. You and your men will have to trace them down."

Captain Jorgens pawed at the wire bristles of his mustache. "I suppose, Simon, that I should be grateful for your pointing out the obvious things as you say. But I am also aware that since you have told me this much, you are several jumps ahead of me on an independent investigation of your own."

"The captain is partially correct," said Crole, savoring his drink. "Our paths run parallel. Only *you* have the responsibility of finding out who murdered James Gillespie."

"Just like that, eh?"

Crole nodded.

"All right. I'll take the responsibility, and plow straight ahead. And if you get in my way, you'll get plowed under. I mean it, Simon. So if your hands are dirty, you'd better start washing up."

"You don't even trust me, do you Captain?"

"Why should I? You don't trust our police department."

Simon Crole rubbed his bald head. "I trust you, Captain. Also your men. They're a fine bunch. You know I do. Your main grievance is that you're peeved because I won't take you fully into my confidence. My business may be linked with crime, but I'm not."

"Tell it to somebody else," snorted Jorgens, reaching for the phone. "Police headquarters," he snapped.

While he waited for the call to be put through he spoke again, "I'm accepting the responsibility right now. Tomorrow you may be only too willing to accept the cooperation of the police department . . .

"Oh hello. Put Sergeant Keeble on the wire. Sergeant, I want you to take a squad car and go out to the spot where the Buick coupe was wrecked on the Iron Mountain grade. Take along Williams and McCarthy. I want pictures of the car's interior, the seat in particular. Also pictures of the road up near the guard rail where the machine went through. Get moving."

He clicked the receiver to the hook and glared at the agency man. "We'll see," he said, grimly, "whether your tip is real or phoney. In the morning I'll start checking Gillespie through his friends and associates. If it's murder—and it must be since you say so—I'll find the guilty man. And I'm sure of plenty of help from the District Attorney's office."

He surged abruptly to his feet.

"Have another drink before you go, Captain," urged Crole, mildly.

"I wouldn't want to rob . . ."

"Wait a second. This liquor is priceless. If you don't want it, say so. I'm not keen about you drinking it up anyways."

"Shut up and pour me a glass."

"After we drink this," said Crole, "I'll ride downtown as far as my office. Just thought of something that'll have to be attended to."

"Get your thinking done tonight, Simon. You may not have a chance tomorrow."

"Think so?"

Captain Jorgen's face was set in grim hardness as he shouldered through the door into the hall, but he said nothing.

Crole followed meekly, absorbed apparently in the building of a cigarette.

Shutting the door carefully and slipping the night latch, Simon Crole snapped on the lights of his office. He looked at his watch. It was two o'clock.

He stood for a minute in the center of his own office while he caught his breath. He never liked the idea of climbing those seven flights of steps during the night, but there was nothing he could do about it. Had he been an ordinary business man and closed up tight at five o'clock, things would have been different.

"What I need," he mused, "is an office on the ground floor. Well, that wouldn't be so good either. Now let me see what our private files have to say about James Gillespie."

He thumbed through the G section. Found Gillespie listed with his business and home address. And that was all he did find. Pursing his lips he turned to the B section in the file.

Here he found without any difficulty the name George Baron. Beneath it was typewritten: "Attorney, spotty reputation, brilliant in court procedure, unscrupulous, unmarried, unethical." And beneath all this was a penciled memorandum in Etta's handwriting: "Also unregenerate."

"Unscrupulous, unethical and unregenerate," repeated Crole. "But these terms would apply to a great many people in this city. Baron didn't kill Gillespie. I think he's too intelligent. But isn't above hiring somebody else to perform his dirty work."

He leaned back in the chair and elevated his feet to the desk top. He thought as he sat there of the lunch he had laid out ready to eat in his apartment. Jorgens' arrival had made him forget his hunger. Now it returned to plague him. He recalled sadly his uneaten food in the coffee shop downstairs. The news of Gillespie's death had caused him to get up from the table and leave it untouched.

He scowled sourly at a lithograph on the wall depicting Darktown's Fire Brigade. What a hell of a thing to have to look at. Mumbling, he took out tobacco sack and papers, rolled a cigarette and glanced warily at his trick lighter. He didn't feel equal to struggling with it, so he used a match.

As the blue smoke curled from his lips and nostrils he thought about Virginia Laird. The thoughts were far from pleasant. That girl knew something. And somebody knew that she knew. If she didn't appear by tomorrow, Crole knew that he would have to show his hand to Captain Jorgens. And that was one thing he didn't want to do.

Thinking of Virginia Laird caused him to remember his visit to Gillespie's office during the afternoon and the piece of cardboard he had tucked away in his pocket.

He turned on a desk lamp and studied it carefully. Something had been written on it with a pencil, then later rubbed out. Opening a desk drawer, the agency man took out a small but powerful microscope, placed the cardboard on the slide and adjusted the lens.

Then shifting the card till it was at an angle he studied the indentation caused by the pressure of the pencil. Shadows filled the depressions and he was able to make out two words: Henry Brenan.

An examination of the opposite side of the cardboard revealed nothing at all.

"Henry Brenan," he wondered aloud. "Now who in the hell is he?"

Concentration wrinkles formed between his eyes. He stared into space as if by an effort of the will he would see everything in its proper relation—one with the other. And all he saw was the miserable lithograph of the Darktown's Fire Brigade.

After a time he yawned, stretched, and thought of his comfortable bed and the cold food on the kitchenette table. He would have gone down to eat in an all-night restaurant, but he didn't relish the walk back upstairs again. Nor did he feel equal to the exertion of hunting a cab and going home.

He tried thinking again about Henry Brenan. But thinking made him sleepy. Grunting with exasperation over hunger and his general laziness about going home, he got to his feet, blinked, snapped off the light, and went over to the leather couch.

His lips puffed out in a thankful sigh as he stretched out. When they had resumed their former shape he was quite sound asleep, one arm beneath his big shoulders, the other hanging limply over the edge.

As Simon Crole slept, the big rotaries of the city presses ground out their columns of scandal, crime, sports and war scares for readers to wonder at over their breakfast coffee.

And while the presses whirled, a man identified as James Gillespie reposed stiffly on a slab in the city morgue. Ned Anderson lay in a drunken stupor surrounded by a choice selection of interesting but empty bottles. George Baron slumbered in a bed with a silken coverlet. Occasionally the muscles of his suave face twitched as if his dreams were tinted with unpleasantness. In a gambling house, where stakes ran high, Gene Selingo and Ghost Mokund waged a losing fight against house percentages from which they were to emerge in the early morning hours flat broke.

The coastal city, otherwise, was sunk in a deep well of sleep.

CHAPTER VII

SECRET FILE

SIMON CROLE WAS AWAKENED by the slamming of a door and a loud yawn. Feet hard-heeled across the floor. Matt Ridley stood beside the leather couch, a cigarette hanging loosely from his lips.

"Geez, boss, did somebody evict you from your apartment?"

"A cigarette, Matt," said Crole, swinging his feet to the floor. "Thanks." He struck a match. The smoke poured into his lungs. It felt good. He took several puffs. "What time is it?" he asked.

"Eight o'clock."

"I'm hungry," said Crole. "Was up most of the night. Too lazy to go home. Seen the papers?"

"Yeah. The police are all hot and bothered. Seems that Gillespie was murdered. They were out to the wreck last night and . . ."

"I know," said Crole. "Had a chin with Jorgens myself last night. We didn't hit it off very well. Did you bring the paper with you? Lemme see it."

Matt took a folded tabloid from his pocket. The news Crole looked for was on the first page. He scanned the headlines briefly.

GILLESPIE VICTIM OF FOUL PLAY

What first appeared an accident according to astute police officials, has definitely been proven a murder.

Crole read the rest of the news item and discovered nothing that he didn't already know. He flung the paper down and got to his feet. Etta was just coming in when he reached her office.

"Morning, precious." He grinned idiotically, for that was the way he felt.

Etta's face was rosily pink. She took off an impudent looking hat, fluffed her hair, looked at Crole sharply, and said: "Boss, you look positively terrible—as if you'd been on a long bender."

"I feel lousy. I slept on the leather couch last night."

"Try sleeping on one of those steel-mattress cots in the jail," said Matt. "I slept on one a couple months back. I'll swear, when I got up my carcass was all marked off with little squares—just like as if I was a waffle."

Crole grunted and picked up the phone. He called a number, waited, then said: "Herman, they's a half-starved man in my office name of Simon Crole who needs a stevedore's breakfast. Send up anything and everything including about a quart of coffee. Bye."

He swung on his operator. "Matt," he said. "Go down to the Commodore. Ask for Ned Anderson. Get the address of Virginia Laird from him. But first find out whether he has learned of her whereabouts. She left Gillespie's office yesterday morning. Now she's missing. I thought for a time she might be with Gillespie. But I reasoned wrong. If she isn't home, try and check her movements through cabs near her office building."

After his operator had left Crole turned to his secretary. "Two long-distance calls, precious, regarding insurance policies on the life of James Gillespie. You're to find out, if possible, the names and addresses of the beneficiaries. The companies are the Oregon Mutual, at Salem I think, and the Guardian Life in New York City. Put the calls in at once."

He started away towards his own office, thought of something and came back. "Call Esther, will you, and connect her with my line."

His former woman operator's voice came over the wire a couple minutes later. "Good morning, Simon. Please be brief. I'm up to my ears in work."

"Listen, darling," purred Crole. "I wish you would move that law office of yours and come over with me. I can rent another room . . ." He twisted his head as a waiter carrying his breakfast entered. "Smells grand . . . No, Esther. Not you. My breakfast. It just arrived. Plutocrat me eye. I was working last night and didn't go home. Yeah, same old blundering Simon. Yeah, I'm on a case. Maybe you read something about it in the newsprints. The Gillespie murder."

He threw a longing glance at the napkin-covered tray. "You'd appreciate the angles, Esther, no foolin'. Well, here's what I want you to do."

"I haven't got time to do anything," protested the girl. "I've got to be in Judge Barnum's court at ten o'clock."

"What I want," said Crole, unperturbed, "is this. Gillespie sold a house out in Los Gatos canyon. I want the name of the purchaser, how much he paid, whether in cash or check. I also want to know if the buyer is living in the house at the present time. If he isn't, then where the hell is he living. You've got friends in the tax assessor's office, and you can trace the payment through the mortgage company that handled the escrow. I wouldn't ask you to do this for me if I could avoid it. But I don't want my name to appear in the investigation."

"You've got a knack Simon," complained the girl over the wire, "of getting your own way. I'll take care of this for you, but understand, under no conditions will I enter this case as an operator."

"You're lovely, Esther. I wish I was younger. I believe I could learn to care for you in a rather—big way."

"Tell it to Etta, you big idiot. The only person you could care for in a really big way, and do, is Simon Crole."

"Mad?"

"Don't be silly, big boy. Bye."

"Bye darling. Be seeing you." He hung up, sighed pleasantly, and reached toward the napkin covering the tray. As he did so he heard the hall door open, then the sound of men's voices. The signal beneath his desk buzzed warningly as Etta pressed her knee against a button below her own desk.

He took down the receiver. "Two gentlemen from the District Attorney's office to see you," said Etta.

Simon Crole grinned crookedly, removed his extended hand from the vicinity of the napkin-covered tray, swore explosively and said: "Send them in."

The two men came in, plainclothes men with broad shoulders, set, rigid faces, their attitudes uncompromising. Crole recognized Daniels and scowled his displeasure.

"All right, Crole," said Daniels. "Get on your hat. The D.A. wants to see you—at once."

"He does, hey—What about?"

"I guess you know all right. Come on. Don't keep us here all morning. We've got other things to do besides hang around a private dick's office."

"I haven't had my breakfast."

"Neither has the D.A."

"Is this a pinch?"

"It will be if you try to put up an argument. Subpoenas are easy to make out. We can take you now with us and have the paper filled out when we get there. Now, do you come, or do we have to get nasty?"

"You guys are always nasty," said Crole, rising. Stopping at Etta's desk on the way out he said: "District Attorney Minifie has something on his mind that requires my presence. So don't worry while Simon is away. I'll get rid of these two big apes in half an hour."

Etta's eyes grew large. "Apes, did you say?"

"Nerts to you, sister," leered Daniels.

"Apes is what I said," repeated Crole, thinly. He opened the door to the hall.

"Wise guy, eh?" sneered Daniels, grimly. "And hardshelled. You may think you're pretty good, Crole, but before Minifie finishes putting you through a course of sprouts, you'll wish you had walked in a straight line. He's been damned easy on you and your methods in the past, but he's got you on ice this time."

Crole had the last word as they waited for the elevator. "When I leave Minifie's office, Daniels, he'll bow me out and apologize for having made an inexcusable error. Mull that over for what comfort you can get out of it."

District Attorney Minifie was an upright, courageous servant of the people. His was a tough job. Between politics, reform groups and crime, he was constantly being enfiladed by the verbal barrages of the press. He was a tireless prosecuting attorney, and what small private life he had was spotlessly correct. He lacked only—the saving grace of humor.

There were dark rings under his eyes, and a sag to his chin from overwork and lack of sleep. He was cross and petulant, and the sight of Simon Crole did little to restore him to an amiable frame of mind.

"Morning, Mr. District Attorney," grinned Crole. "Mind sending the escort away? They get on my nerves. A telephone call would have accomplished the same thing."

"Sit down, Crole," said the district attorney, wearily. He waved his men from the room.

"Now," he resumed, turning tired eyes on the agency man. "I'm afraid you've slipped badly, Crole, this time. Captain Jorgens discovered last night that James Gillespie was murdered. Between our different offices we've been carrying on an investigation. You were interested in Gillespie—obscure reasons of your own most likely."

"Very obscure."

"What we lack, Crole, is a reasonable motive for Gillespie being murdered. We believe you know the motive. As a matter of cold fact, Crole, we have every reason to believe that your office is mixed up in this killing."

Crole found something interesting in the palm of his hand that apparently needed looking at. While examining it he said: "The fact that you immediately suspect me of being linked with this crime, Minifie, is quite usual in your office and does not interest me. What does interest me, however," he went on, looking the prosecutor squarely in the eyes, "is the method you used to arrive at a wrong conclusion."

"An unknown man phoned my office, Crole. He said he saw you enter and leave the building yesterday afternoon where James Gillespie has, or rather had his office. An elevator operator remembered seeing you and another man enter the office where you remained for perhaps half an hour. I showed the operator your picture. He said there couldn't be a mistake."

"I've got a face that people don't easily forget," said Crole.

"Gillespie's safe was open," continued Minifie, "and from a casual examination made by Captain Jorgens' men and my own, it would seem that its interior had been thoroughly looted."

"You really think that I opened and robbed that safe, Minifie?"

"You had another man with you."

"So I did. Well, go on with the indictment. I'd like to hear the rest. One of your men told me that you had me on ice. But it looks like the ice is melting."

"You admit, then, that you were in Gillespie's office . . ."

"Listen, Minifie. I was in that office with another man. The safe was open. Nobody was around—or so I thought. I was interested in the place. So I did a little looking around. James Gillespie was a man I especially desired to see right then. You can imagine what a shock I received when I learned of his accident on the Iron Mountain grade."

"Don't try to be funny, Crole. Your humor is rather out of place under the circumstances, and I thoroughly disapprove your treating murder as something of no special significance."

"I stand corrected, Mr. District Attorney. But I still insist that I was shocked when I learned of the accidental death of James Gillespie. And that's no joke."

The District Attorney leaned forward in his chair. Color spotted his cheeks. Personal animosity got the better of him. Suppressed rage caused his eyes to flame redly.

"Now listen here, Crole. I've stood for all I'm going to from you. You've flouted the law, suppressed information, and been underhanded in your business ethics. But I've reached the limit of my endurance. I'm going to crush you, Crole. And I'm going to begin by seeing to it that your license as a private detective is taken away from you."

Crole said mildly: "I didn't know you were so vindictive, Mr. District Attorney."

"I'm not. I'm just downright angry."

"That's unfortunate. Very. And I'm sorry you feel that way, Minifie, for I know from experience how easy it is to fall into error."

"Then you understand a damn sight more than I do," raged the District Attorney. "For a single thin dime, I'd slap you in a cell where nobody could get to you. And I'd hold you there as long as the law allows me. And believe me, you'd come out a chastened man, ready to talk—not hinder public investigations."

Crole tossed a dime to Minifie's desk. "I'm calling you."

"Damn sure of yourself, aren't you?"

"If you'd get a grip on yourself, Minifie, I'll explain you a few things for your own good."

"All right. Sorry for the outburst of bad temper. But I'm being harassed from all sides."

"Do you know who put Captain Jorgens on the murder angle of what looked like an ordinary accident?"

"Sergeant Keeble, along with the fingerprint and picture experts, Williams and McCarthy."

"Wrong."

"You calling me a liar?"

"I said you were wrong. If Jorgens forgot to tell you, that's no fault of mine. I went out and investigated the wreck myself. Afterwards I called the captain on the phone and told him that it was murder. He came to my apartment breathing fire. I almost had to draw a diagram to convince him as to why I thought it *was* murder. Figure it out, Minifie. Would I do all this if I was involved in a killing?"

"I don't think you would, Crole. But you're a peculiar individual, with deeper recesses in your mind than most men."

"I'll tell you something else, Minifie. You said an unknown man called your office and told you he had seen me
enter the building. It might be just possible that this unknown
was the same mug who was hiding in a storeroom in Gillespie's office while I was there. He cracked me over the head
when I opened the door. Did the same thing to the gentleman
who was with me. Neither of us got a look at his face." The
district attorney's eyes registered unbelief. Crole pointed to
the welt on the side of his head now bluish in color. "You
still don't believe me. All right. Listen some more. The man
who was with me in Gillespie's office was also struck with
the same weapon. His name is Ned Anderson. He's registered at the Commodore."

"Mind telling me why you were there?"

Simon Crole shrugged. "Why not?" Deftly he rolled a cigarette. "Anderson has been abroad for over two years. Before
he left, he placed his funds in Gillespie's hands for investment, giving him power of attorney.

"When Anderson returned he found out through the bank
that his account of over two hundred thousand dollars had
shriveled to nothing. He came to me seeking help. Together
we went to Gillespie's office. He wasn't there. The place
was open. He wasn't at his apartment. Couldn't be found
anywhere until . . ."

Minifie raised a deprecatory hand. "I don't like this business, Crole. You're altogether too glib." He rubbed tired
eyes with his fingers. "You can go, Crole—but not out of
town."

"Why should I leave town. My business is here. There's
nothing for me to worry about, and you ought to know it by
this time."

"Oh, get out of here. The sight of your face makes me
sick."

Crole got to his feet. "I feel sick, too, Minifie—same reason."

A block from the building housing the District Attorney's office, Crole entered a telephone booth and called Anderson.

"Crole talking," he said quietly. "Listen. I just came from the District Attorney's office. He would have given anything to have linked me with Gillespie's killing. He'll be looking you up sometime this morning. You can tell him all you want to except one angle. Forget about Virginia Laird and her visit to you leading up to the attempted kidnapping. Clear? Remember, not a word. I have my own reasons. Swell, and try to keep sober. Bye."

Etta smiled brightly as he entered the office. "I see you got rid of them apes."

"Yeah," sighed Crole. "They're gone. For good, too, I hope. Now, maybe, I can get around to getting some food inside me."

"What did Minifie want of the gun?"

"Gun?" Crole's eyebrows moved up. "Did you say gun, precious?"

"That's what I said. The man who came for it told me . . ."

"You foolish kid," interrupted Crole, grimly aware of a warning tinkle of a bell somewhere in the center of his brain. "You shouldn't have given it to him—or anybody else."

Etta's face blanched. Sudden realization of what she had done caused her lips to quiver. "Boss," she said, her voice no longer bland, but on the actual point of breaking. "You mean that I . . .?"

Crole didn't blame the girl. The trick was an old one. He had used it himself, in various ways. But it made him wince to have someone use it on him.

"Somebody pulled a fast one on you, girl. I never sent anyone for my gun. There was no reason why I should."

"But he told me that the District Attorney . . ."

"Whatever he told you was a lie. I never sent anyone . . ." He broke off suddenly. His eyes swerved. They came to rest on the hall door. It was opening slowly, almost imperceptibly.

And revealed in the opening stood a man—a man whose face was deathly gray. The lips of this man were moving, but no sound was coming from them.

Etta suddenly clutched Crole by the arm. "Boss," she half sobbed. "It's him. He's the man—the same man who came in while you were away and got your gun."

Simon Crole took two steps forward and froze. His eyes lighted with recognition. The man in the doorway was Coughlin, the private detective.

He was swaying on his feet now like a reed in a gale. And his throat was making a rasping sound as if his wind pipes were coated with sand.

His fingers clutched the front of his coat, the knuckles of his hand showing white like tiny islands on a background of tan.

Crole kicked the door shut and placed a supporting arm in the small of Coughlin's back. Something told him that Coughlin was going to die—here in his office.

A thin trickle of dark liquid struck the office floor and splattered flatly. Crole looked again at the clenched hand holding the coat tight against the man's body. The fingers were beginning to relax, and with the lessening of those fingers the flood, no longer held back, streamed from the underside of Coughlin's coat, and smeared the floor in a reddish, drumming patter.

"Get a doctor, precious!" snapped Crole. "Doctor Cane. No, don't bother with the phone. Run down to the third floor and bring him back with you. Scram, little one!"

He stood for a moment, after the girl had fled, looking moody and depressed. Again that faint tinkle of a bell was sounding in his brain. A warning signal. Disaster was close. How was he to avoid it?

Groaning, Coughlin slid from Crole's supporting arm into a bloody heap on the floor.

CHAPTER VIII

ASTUTE OFFICIALS

WITH SURPRISING GENTLENESS, Simon Crole gathered the dying man into his cradled arms and fixed him as comfortably as possible on the leather couch in his own office. Then he poured a small amount of whiskey in a glass and held it to the doomed man's lips.

"Get this into you, Coughlin," he urged. "It'll help." Coughlin's dry lips scraped against the rim of the glass. Crole held him in a partially upright position. Convulsively he swallowed. Then his head sagged loosely and his eyes closed.

Kneeling beside the unfortunate man Crole said: "Who did it, Coughlin? Who shot you?"

The eyes of Coughlin opened. Already a thin film was beginning to glaze them. His lips moved in a husky whisper. Crole missed the first half dozen words. All he heard was " . . . from Lima, Ohio. Edward Smith . . . double for Gillespie . . . girl suspects . . . snatch . . . checked . . . warn against . . . you . . . gun . . . frame . . . the rat! Turns gun on me . . . get him . . ." The husky whisper trailed into a harsh swirl of an indrawn breath.

"Who?" insisted Crole, bending close. "Who shot you, Coughlin? Tell me. I'll see that he gets what's coming to him."

The convulsion started deep, racking the wounded man with paralyzing twinges of pain. His lips moved— soundlessly. No word issued from the dry lips, nothing but a slow exhale of the last breath Coughlin would ever breathe.

Simon Crole, still kneeling, saw the last flicker of life in the eyelids, then before his eyes, the dead man seemed to turn into wax—so still was he.

For several long moments Crole did nothing but stare into the face of the murdered man as if hypnotized. He knew, as well as he knew anything, that the death of this man on the leather couch was linked somehow with the murder of James Gillespie.

But how? What part had Coughlin played? Was he the man who had tried to kidnap Virginia Laird? Was he the man who had hidden in the storeroom? And why had he come here and talked Etta out of the gun, only to return a few minutes later mortally wounded?

Simon Crole straightened. His eyes were sink holes of despair. He looked carefully around the office. Listened for the sound of footsteps in the hall. Licked his lips during a split second of indecision, then bent over the dead man.

Expertly he went through Coughlin's pockets, keeping his fingers away from everything metallic. In the breast coat pocket he found a folded square of paper. He spread it open, read: "Secret File, Ask Leahy." Scurrying footsteps in the hall warned him that Etta was returning.

He slid the paper to his own pocket and stepped back from the body, not looking towards the front office.

Through the door came Etta, her dress rustling. Behind her followed Dr. Cane. As the doctor came through the door his foot kicked something on the floor, and sent it against the partition in back of Etta's desk.

Simon Crole left the body of the dead man. Etta and the doctor, both, were looking at that lump of metal on the floor. Crole looked. His lips twisted, and the look of perpetual surprise was on his face. Only this time it was real—the lump of metal was his gun—a Luger equipped with a silencer that had been clamped on by somebody other than himself.

Doctor Cane's eyes swung from the gun on the floor to the man on the leather couch. In them was a double question.

"I think you're too late, Doc," said Crole, shaking his bald head. "The man's dead."

As Doctor Cane bent to examine the body on the couch, Etta started to retrieve the Luger and was brought to sudden immobility by Crole's: "Leave it!" Her eyes held worried glints as they looked in his. Reassuringly, he laid a big hand on her shoulders. And his voice deep and purring sought to ease the tension in her young body. "Don't let it get you down, precious. Not for a minute. The frame was timed beautifully, but it isn't going to work. Not this time. Your lips, kid. Turn 'em up at the corners. That's better. Everything's gonna be all right."

"I hardly think," said Doctor Cane, dryly, "that you'll find it quite as simple as you seem to think, Crole. This man has been shot through the vital organs—apparently in your office. There's blood all over the floor—and what looks like the murder weapon."

"I noticed the gun," said Crole, mildly amused, "and I've been trying to figure how it got there on the floor. Things sure look bad. Very bad. Especially for me, since that's my gun on the floor." He turned to the girl.

"Turn in the alarm, precious. Call Police Captain Jorgens. Oh!" He placed a protecting arm around the girl's shoulders and led her to the nearest window which he jerked upward.

"Sorry, kid. I didn't realize you were getting sick. Here, sit down. Stick your head out the window and get some fresh air. You'll be all right in a second. Now get control of yourself while I get the police mob on our premises. Your boss is gonna be grilled, and grilled plenty."

He sighed morosely as he reached for the phone. "Damn it. I hope the time is coming soon when I can sit down in peace and eat. I don't mind working for my fees, but I never figured on starving myself to death. One meal is all I ask. Geez, it seems like so little, but I don't seem to have a Chinaman's chance of getting it. Police Headquarters," he finished, sadly. "Captain Jorgens."

George Baron, ensconced in a beautiful mahogany chair in his impressive office, heard the muted tingling of the inter-office phone, ran exploring fingers over his perfectly-groomed hair, lifted the receiver from its cradle, and said:

"Well?" The receiver crackled as the secretary in the waiting room explained certain matters.

Baron was breathing rather rapidly as if he had just passed through some great emotional stress. He didn't want to be bothered at this time. He needed isolation where he could think. There were many and varied things that had called and were still to call for intense concentration—none of them directly connected with his court work.

"Who are they?" he asked.

"They won't give their names. They just grin and look wise. I think, Mr. Baron, you had better see them."

George Baron knew, then, who his callers were. Being a smart lawyer, instinctively cunning, and an opportunist of the first rank, he had no physical fear of these two men who, he had supposed, had left the coastal city for points east.

He would have to have help with his many and varied things. These men had proved capable. Perhaps he could make further use of them. Yes, it would be wise on his part to cultivate these men, to use them. The time was surely coming when . . .

"Show them in," he told his secretary. "Then you can take the rest of the day off. I won't need you." He hung up, adjusted his smile, then allowed pleased surprise to cross his face as Ghost Mokund and Gene Selingo shuffled into the room. He motioned them to chairs, saw his secretary leave the office, then quietly closed the door and locked it.

Ghost Mokund's hands were deep in his coat pockets when Baron came back into the room. Selingo was fidgeting uneasily, a vacant look staring out of his face.

"Don't be alarmed, boys," said George Baron, suavely. "I sent the girl home, and locked the door to keep out unwelcome callers. Glad to see you again, of course, but I thought—I thought you would be fairly well on your way east by this time."

Mokund grunted.

Selingo wiped the vacant look from his face. "Well, we didn't go. Decided to hang around this town for a couple days. Last night we was taken for our roll in a gyp gambling joint. They cleaned us pretty and I still can't figure it out. Other guys were hitting the house for plenty. But us—we got nothing but a headache." George Baron nodded. "That's the way things go." He reached for his checkbook. "Broke?"

"Yeah," said Selingo.

"A thousand see you through?"

Mokund lighted a cigarette. His boy face was expressionless. He dragged deeply on the burning tobacco. "Yeeeah!" he yawned.

Selingo said: "I don't like checks."

"I'll go with you to the bank and get the cash. Will you be leaving, or do you boys want to work for me?"

"Doing what?" asked Selingo.

"Various things," said Baron. He took a lean cigar from a box on his desk, clipped it with sharp front teeth, held a match to it and watched Selingo's face register in turn pleasure and greed.

"Sure, we'll work for you. Why not? What'll it be, straight pay by the day, or commission?"

"Either way."

"Jobs like the last one aren't as easy as they look. You know that, Baron."

"I know that."

"Five thousand is little enough. We need more for handling that kind of work. Understand, we ain't trying to chisel in on your racket, whatever it is. It's just that the cops are gonna be all hot and bothered. You read the papers?"

George Baron nodded. "Naturally."

"Well?"

"Well, what?"

"This town has got smarter dicks than I thought. Somebody told me they were only a bunch of hicks. Somebody lied. Ghost and me will have to give this town the air if things begin to get hot."

"You can leave with the thousand cash now, boys, or you can stick around and make considerably more. You know the risks, However," he added, studying the ash forming on his cigar, "I don't anticipate much trouble from the police. I

have every reason to believe that a certain individual in this
city who might cause us trouble, has been or will soon be
eliminated from the scene."

"Who the hell you got in mind?" asked Selingo.

"I'll tell you who he is later," said Baron, "after we have
reached a working agreement with each other. In the meantime, I think we had better call at the bank. You boys must
need money."

"Yeah?" Gene Selingo's big mouth slitted into a wide grin.
"Maybe you think we don't know it, hey?"

"Ummmm!" grunted Ghost Mokund, crushing his cigarette.

The pen of George Baron moved swiftly across the face of
a check made out to cash. He tore it from the book, tucked it
in his pocket. "We'll go down to the bank now," he said.

"Why should we?" said Selingo, mistaking Baron's suave
exterior for something it was not.

The eyes of George Baron began to retreat into the back of
his skull. A sudden tautness drew his lips into a thin leer of
contempt. "Listen," he said in a thin, steely voice. "We
might as well get our relations with each other straightened
out. You men will work for me. You'll obey my orders. And
I'll pay you damned well—in cash. Otherwise, no dice."

Selingo said: "You needn't get sore."

"My eyes are wide open," said George Baron. "I know
where I'm going. I ask only loyalty and obedience. Take it or
leave it. What will it be?"

"We'll stick with you," said Selingo, after a moment of
swift thinking. "I gotta hunch you're a right guy. How do
you feel, Ghost?"

Mokund looked as if he might grunt, flipped a cigarette between his lips, lit it, inhaled and said: "Oke."

The tension relaxed. George Baron led the way downstairs
to the bank. The other two men followed, subdued and silent.

Simon Crole sat behind his desk, feet elevated to its top,
hands crossed over the center button of his coat. There was

neither fear nor elation in his round face—merely a tolerance for the wild confusion that swirled in and out of his office.

Captain Jorgens with a couple of radio car cops was looking down at the stiffening body of Coughlin. Daniels and the other investigator from the District Attorney's office—the same two whom Crole had christened apes—were standing close to the hall door, their hands suspiciously close to their hip pockets. There was an "I knew this was bound to happen" expression on their faces. And they were prepared to start shooting if Simon Crole made any movement to leave his office.

Two flash guns popped blindingly as the photographic experts took pictures of the dead man. They popped a second time in the general direction of the blood-smeared floor and carpet.

The medical examiner, a thin man with myopic eyes and a ghastly sense of humor, came through the door carrying a black bag. A happy man, the examiner, on whose shoulders the tribulations of mankind rested lightly.

"Greetings, gentlemen, greetings," he bowed. "How are you, Captain Jorgens? And you, gentlemen of the press. I should have arrived earlier. My car broke down. It's always breaking down." He rubbed his hands briskly. "And the cadaver. Where is . . .?"

"Over there, Doctor," pointed one of the cops.

"Ummmm. So it is. So it is." He bent over the body, pulled back eyelids, felt of the hollow in the dead man's neck, then at the pulse, and finally turned back the blood-smeared coat.

Everybody started talking at once. A reporter had grabbed up the phone and was trying to reach his city editor. Out in the front office another reporter was sitting on the desk and trying to make Etta talk.

"Leave me alone," snapped the girl.

"Standoffish, hey? Think you're a wise gal. That the line?"

Etta recovered her bland smile, used it, said: "On your way, scandalmonger. Nobody asked you inside."

"Try and keep me out. Listen, baby. I got what it takes to put janes like you in their place. You won't get anywhere with me taking that attitude. You'll talk and talk plenty . . ."

Simon Crole had risen to his feet as their voices reached his ears. Abruptly he sighed, relaxed. He saw Matt Ridley's homely face coming through the front door.

The reporter snarled as a vise-like hand clomped down on his shoulder, swung him around and lifted him bodily from the desk.

"Don't get fresh with the office help," said Matt. "And if you have to sit, use a chair. Otherwise stand up—on the floor."

The reporter jerked his shoulder from Matt's hand. His eyes were cloudy, his mouth crooked. Ridley spoke quietly: "Don't say it. It won't help you, and it might make me mad."

He sat down in the spot vacated by the reporter and flung a quick glance around him. "Looks, kid, like the place is pinched. Boss in his office?"

Etta nodded. Rapidly she told him everything that had happened. He sat quiet, apparently unmoved and mildly interested. And the investigation continued.

"Dead less than an hour," said the medical examiner, "of a bullet wound through the upper abdominal wall inflicted by person or persons unknown. A small trace of whiskey on lips and chin. How much inside I don't know. An autopsy would show." He turned on Police Captain Jorgens. "Where'd it happen, in this room?"

Jorgens scowled. "I don't know. He died here. He may have been shot here. That's what I'll have to find out."

"Well, that's your job, not mine. I'll make out a murder ticket, but it could be suicide. Simon," he grinned at the private detective, "you're an intelligent man, and you know more about what happened than the rest of us. How do you figure it?"

"You hit it the first time," shrugged Crole.

"Then it's murder, Captain," said the examiner. "Take it from me, it's murder. Crole should know. Simon, you're on the spot. Excuse the levity. Knock, knock! Who's there? Police. Police who? Po-lice get the hell out of here. Well, I'm going. Nothing more I can do here. I'll examine the cadaver later on, Captain, if . . ."

"I don't think it will be necessary," said investigator Daniels, portentously. "Coughlin was killed by a slug from Crole's Luger. Here in this office, by all the signs."

Two internes in white jackets came in with a stretcher. The body of Coughlin was placed upon it and carried out. The fingerprint man was wrapping the Luger in a handkerchief. Photographers were milling around for additional shots. And the news-hawks waited for handouts.

"Clear the office, Captain," said Crole, wearily. "You put on a good show. I got a good laugh out of the medical examiner, and a pain in the neck at Daniels' ugly suspicion. Keep Daniels here with you and send the rest of the mob home. Otherwise we'll get nowhere."

The rabble had quitted the agency office. Simon Crole sat behind his desk. Beside him was Etta. Across from him were Captain Jorgens and Daniels, representing the District Attorney's office.

"Now," Crole was saying, "I was down in Minifie's office, as Daniels already knows. I left there and came directly here."

"You stopped and made a phone call," corrected Daniels.

"So I did. I had forgotten."

Jorgens coughed. "About this Luger, Simon?"

"I'm getting to it. But while I was away—all right, Etta. Tell Captain Jorgens what happened while I was out of the office."

Etta told him.

"Hmmmm!" grunted Jorgens. "Coughlin comes in, wrangles the gun from your secretary. Goes away. Then later returns to your office and dies from a bullet wound caused by your own gun."

"That's my story, Captain," insisted Crole, "and I'll stick to it. But I'm not laying claim to the silencer. That was clamped on while in Coughlin's possession."

"You insisted," said Jorgens, "that Coughlin, though mortally wounded, came into your office alone and unaided, and rather disagreeably croaks on you?"

"Exactly."

Captain Jorgens pawed at the bristles of his mustache. "That ought to be easy to check, since he must have come up on one of the three elevators."

"I was hoping you'd get around to this angle," said Crole. "It struck me right away that a man in Coughlin's condition would attract attention the second he entered an elevator. And the operator would be sure to remember his actions and face."

Captain Jorgens turned to Daniels. "You're not in my department, Daniels. And I can't tell you what to do. But if you want to get hold of the elevator men and take them down to view the body, it might help both our departments."

"Sure," said Daniels. "I'll take care of it."

After the investigator had left, Jorgens fastened his bleak eyes on the private detective. "Maybe you'll talk, now that we're alone. How and where did Coughlin fit in? And what's your quarrel with him?"

"No quarrel," said Crole, "that I know of. But I think I have a notion that he's linked with the murder of James Gillespie."

"Any tangible reason for this quaint notion?"

"Nope. It's just something that's in the air."

"As usual, Simon, you tell me what you want me to know, but you never tell me all you know."

"You're pretty good yourself, Captain, when it comes to holding things back."

"What's your grievance, Simon?"

"Wasn't I the one who pointed out that the man your office identified as Gillespie was murdered?"

"Yeah. Sure!"

Crole nodded. "I didn't mind, Captain, your office getting credit for being, as the papers expressed it: 'Astute officials.' That part's okay with me. You take the glory. Me—I'll take my fees. But since you gave Minifie the impression of having uncovered the murder yourself, it placed me in a bad light. And Minifie was convinced till I argued him out of his notion that I murdered Gillespie."

"I'm sorry," said Jorgens. "But the police and the district attorney's departments are separate. And there's bound to be misunderstandings."

"Which explains why I prefer to work alone."

"By God, Crole!" raged the police captain. "You'll work with me hereafter, or I'll know . . ."

The telephone rang. Etta started to reach for it. "I'll take it," said Crole. "Hello," he called. "Oh! Fine, darling. But keep it till some other time. Simon's busy. Believe it or not, a man was practically murdered in my office. Call me tonight. Call me at supper time. We'll have dinner together. It's been nearly two days since I've had so much as a smell of food. Right. Bye."

"Or I'll know," continued Jorgens, "the reason why."

"I forgot what it was you were saying," said Crole, rolling a cigarette.

Captain Jorgens swore crossly.

"Dear me," said Etta. "If you'll excuse me, Captain, I'll go back to my desk."

"Yarrrgh!" choked Jorgens, pounding the desk with his fist. "You've got everybody trained around here."

"The young lady," explained Crole, patiently, "objects to the Captain's swearing. She's a genteel person. Hell! She won't let me get away with it. Why should she make you an exception?"

Captain Jorgens found a broken cigar in his pocket, eyed it moodily and clamped it between his teeth. "Well," he growled, lifting his bulk erect. "We're agreed on one thing. Coughlin was murdered." He walked to the window and stood looking outside.

"That's something," said Crole, pouring himself a glass of Bourbon.

Ridley came sidling out of his cubby-hole of a room and sat down in the chair vacated by Etta. He said nothing. He didn't have to. Crole knew why he was there and what he wanted. "Help yourself," he said. Which Matt Ridley did with neatness and dispatch. The police captain, hearing the tinkle of glass and gurgle of liquid, heaved around with red-eyed exasperation, muttered beneath his breath, and again turned his eyes to the contemplation of the buildings outside the window.

CHAPTER IX

MURDER TO COME

DANIELS, THE INVESTIGATOR from the District Attorney's office, came back into the room swaggering with importance. On his face there was a knowing smile of satisfaction in a duty well done.

"I took all three of the elevator operators down to the morgue, Captain Jorgens, and let them look at Coughlin's body. And not a single one remembered bringing him up allowing that he was in bad shape from the mortal wound. And there wasn't a drop of blood in any of their cars."

Captain Jorgens sucked in a deep breath like a swimmer going into action. Here was something tangible into which he could sink his molars. And he was prepared, mentally, to bite deep.

His voice was no longer petulant with exasperation. It was strong and deep—the voice of a police officer sure of his ground.

"Well, Simon, it looks like you almost got away with murder. Daniels is an ace investigator. He knows his stuff. His report, backed by the testimony of the elevator operators, is likely to prove more convincing than your story. Your facts don't check—not by a long shot. As I see it, there's only one thing for me to do under the circumstances. I am going to charge you with the murder of Coughlin. There's no other way out for me."

"Listen, Captain," said Crole. "You aren't prepared to arrest me. Neither is Daniels. The fact that Coughlin wasn't observed in the elevators doesn't make out a case against me. As a matter of fact it strengthens a hunch I have been nursing for the last couple of hours."

"Save your breath," Daniels snapped. "You're sunk."

Jorgen's eyes clouded with vague, disturbing doubts. He knew Simon Crole better than most men. Knew his weaknesses. And by the same token—knew and respected his strength. Knew that Crole was one of those rare individuals who become progressively better as the situations around him become worse.

The police captain's inclination was to cut the investigation short and take Crole with him to headquarters on any kind of a technical charge. But his better judgment argued against any such move. For this officer sensed, deep within him, that Simon Crole must have an ace card tucked away inside that bald head of his, waiting to play it only at the last minute. Bitter experiences out of the past warned him to go slow.

Simon Crole's lips twitched in their surprised smile. "Listen patiently, Captain—you, too, Daniels, to what I have to submit in the reconstruction of this crime."

"No need for reconstruction," said Daniels. "It's all plain enough. Don't you agree with me, Captain Jorgens?"

Jorgens did not agree, but did not say so. He merely said: "Let him talk. Many a suspect has talked his way into a labyrinth that ended in complete confession. Say what you've got to say, Simon. We'll listen."

"Fair enough," said Crole. "Here's an angle I want you to consider. While I was at the District Attorney's office, two men, we'll say, came up in the elevator at different periods and got off at this floor where they met. One of them, Coughlin, came into my office knowing I was not here, and why.

"He secured my gun by telling my secretary that District Attorney Minifie had sent him for it. Believing him, my secretary gave him the weapon, and he left my office.

"Somewhere on this same floor he again met the man who came with him. This man fitted a silencer to the gun's barrel—not in the hall, but in some empty room or office. There may be an empty office on this floor. I don't know. I *do* know, however, that there is a men's washroom. The lock to the door has been broken for the past week, which the manager of the building or the janitor can testify to.

"Assume under this hypothesis that the unknown of these two men attempted to force Coughlin to do something he did not want to do."

"You're assuming too damn much," snorted Jorgens, "and you know it."

"Coughlin," resumed Crole, smoothly, "was a private detective like myself. He knew his limitations as such. But let's assume again, for the moment, that Coughlin figured he had gone plenty far in obtaining my gun under false pretensions and was unwilling to further incriminate himself in this other man's schemes."

Captain Jorgens took up the story thread unwillingly. "They get into an argument," he stated, "and the argument ends in a fight. And since the unknown man has the gun, poor Coughlin is the one who takes the bullet in his belly."

"Right," grunted Crole, wagging his head with appreciation. "Now, Daniels," he continued, "will you check what I have suggested? Examine the hall outside for traces of blood. Try all the office doors without firm names on the panels—and Daniels, don't overlook the washroom."

Daniels flung a sharp glance at the police captain.

"Go ahead," said Jorgens, defiantly. "It won't take you more than five minutes."

In less than five minutes the investigator was back in the office. There was no longer a look of satisfaction on his face. His mouth was slightly out of line, and there was a queer, tight expression in his eyes.

"There's blood in the hall, small spots. The man who spilled that blood came down the hall from the washroom to Crole's door. Some of the spots have small teeth at their edges, others are shaped like exclamation points. And they indicate the direction the wounded man was moving quite accurately. But—Crole might have done the shooting in the washroom and afterwards . . ."

"I suppose," interrupted Crole, "that it's your business to solve crimes. It happens to be mine, too. But how about the gun? Would I leave it kicking around my office floor? Wouldn't it have been simpler for me to have left Coughlin in the washroom rather than bring him down the hall into my office, then obligingly incriminate myself by leaving the murder weapon on the floor?"

"All this argument is getting us nowhere," said Captain Jorgens.

"All right," agreed Crole. "Take me down to headquarters. Lock me up in a cell. Charge me with murder and see how far you get with your investigation. And while I'm locked up what do you suppose will happen?"

The eyes of Captain Jorgens slitted. "You tell *me*."

Simon Crole stared at the police officer, past him, and his eyes focused once more on the lithograph of the Darktown Fire Brigade. Hunger gnawed at his vitals. His eyes swerved downward to the leather couch where Coughlin had died.

Memory re-created the scene. The moving lips whispering huskily. The pain-racked eyes. Broken words—incoherent for the most part. Yet they meant something. They formed a picture with lines running in all directions like the spokes of a wheel. Could those lines be straightened, joined together in their ordered sequence, the incoherency would vanish. And out of the rush of broken words would emerge the final picture—crystal clear in every detail.

In the light of what he already knew, the pendulum that represented human greed had not yet swung its full arc. Its movement would accelerate before it would slow up at the terminal of its oscillation. And Crole sensed instinctively that this terminal had not yet been reached—would not be reached until another man had died. Somewhere in this incompleted picture of greed was a man by the name of Edward Smith.

The fan-wise wrinkles arching outward from the corners of Simon Crole's eyes slowly deepened. His lips twitched, and he said quietly: "There is yet another murder to come. And nothing any of us can do will stop it."

"Even with you in jail?"

"In spite of it, Captain."

"He's nuts!" clipped Daniels.

Captain Jorgens pawed at the bristles of his mustache, shifted the cigar wedged between his teeth, glared at nobody in particular, said: "We're all nuts, and just a shade removed from idiocy. A man brings Coughlin to Simon Crole's door. Shoots him in the belly, pushes him inside . . ."

"Coughlin borrowed the gun first," corrected the agency man.

"What does it matter? Coughlin comes staggering through the door, and the murderer chucks the weapon in after him. And nobody—neither you, Crole, nor your secretary—has the remotest idea who the killer was or how he got the gun on your office floor."

"He must have opened the door," said Crole, "while Etta was down on the third floor getting Doctor Cane."

"And you didn't hear him?"

"No. I was busy making Coughlin comfortable." Captain Jorgens shrugged. "Let it go at that. But the investigation will go on. I'll have Coughlin's murderer under lock and key within twenty-four hours, or *I'll* turn in my badge."

He turned on Daniels. "I'm going back to headquarters to see what the experts have turned up in the way of prints on that gun. Coming along?"

Daniels flung a swift glance at Crole. Saw only a slumped figure behind the desk, smiled knowingly and said: "Sure, why not?"

Together they left the office, and peace reigned once more.

Simon Crole snapped erect the moment they were out of sight, reached for the phone, changed his mind and turned to Matt Ridley, who had sat through the grilling without saying a single word.

"What did you find out, Matt?"

"I found Anderson in the hotel. He was sad and quite drunk. I got Virginia Laird's address out of him, took a couple of drinks and left him stretched out in a dress suit on the bed.

"Out on the street I grabs a cab and goes out to see Virginia's mother. A swell old dame. She wasn't worried. A telegram had come early in the morning from Kansas City. Virginia is on her way to New York by plane. Special business for her boss, James Gillespie."

"Odd," observed Crole, looking at his watch. "But I was offered twenty thousand dollars if I would go to New York, too."

"Geez!" gasped Matt. "That's a lot of dough."

"It hurt me to turn the offer down."

"Hurt you? I should think it would paralyze you. Whyn't you snap it up?"

"Reasons," said Crole, "too numerous to mention. I figured, also, that someone wanted to get rid of me quickly. And I didn't want to be gotten rid of."

"That's as good a reason as any," agreed Ridley.

"Speaking about planes," said Crole, "you'll be taking one tonight, Matt. You will go to Lima, Ohio. You will search the various records of that town and find out all you can about a certain individual named Edward Smith. Etta will give you expense money. As soon as your report is ready, phone it to me."

Matt Ridley beamed. "Swell. I ain't been in a plane since I closed that case in Yuma. Edward Smith, huh. Who the hell is he?"

"Stupid," said Crole. "Do you suppose I'd waste good money sending you east by plane if I knew who he was? Find out for yourself and phone me."

Matt Ridley left, humming the latest swing tune. Etta came into Crole's office sometime later. She had on her hat and coat. In her hand was a penciled memorandum.

"It looks like you're going places," observed Crole.

"I'm going home," said Etta. "I've had enough of this madhouse for one day."

"But you're coming back?" Crole really looked alarmed. "You . . ."

"Of course I'm coming back—tomorrow. But I'm through for today. I'm all tight inside."

"You had me scared for a minute, precious. I thought you were quitting your job." He cupped the palms of his hands against his eyes. "I wish I was tight. I wish I . . . Honest to God, kid, do you realize how close I am to actual starvation?"

"Want me to send up something from Herman's?"

"No, I guess not. I'll go down . . ."

"You look seedy, boss, and in need of a shave. Esther called while you were having the last and final argument with the captain. You're to pick her up at seven o'clock at her home."

"Seven o'clock," mused Crole. "That's a long time to wait for my dinner. I don't know whether I can hold out till then or not. But you run along, precious. You stood up swell under everything. And I'm proud you work for me instead of somebody else. What's that paper in your hand?"

"It's a report on the insurance policies you asked me to get information on."

"Good girl," taking the paper from her hand. "Now run along. Scram!"

Etta waved him an airy kiss from the doorway. "That's for being a brave man while all those horrid people were insisting you murdered that man."

An amused smile lighted Crole's face. "Brave? Kid, I was scared witless for fear that they actually *would* pin the murder rap on me."

The door closed behind her rustling dress. He heard her heels tapping out jaunty steps in the corridor, the clang of the elevator door, then blessed silence dropped over his office.

He poured himself a drink and sipped it slowly. After the glass was empty he constructed a cigarette, and, still wary of the trick lighter used a match instead. Then leaned back in his chair to scan the insurance report.

"Item one," he read: "The Guardian Life of New York have never issued a policy, either life or accident insurance, to James Gillespie."

Crole whistled softly and his mind went winging back to the dank chamber of the lost dead. Once again he was hearing the voice of the morgue attendant recounting the description of the two men who posed as representatives of the Guardian Life. 'Only one of them talked. The other just grunted. The one who grunted had a funny face—like a boy's. Smooth. No wrinkles. But he wasn't a boy. The other had a face like yours—kinda round. His lips were thicker than yours and he had a big mouth.'

"Hmmmm!" thought Crole. "Easy to recognize if I only knew where to look for them. And that would be a job. I think I'll turn that part over to the police. They're better equipped to find these two men than I am."

He turned to the paper in his hand and read: "Item two: The Oregon Mutual Insurance Company have a twenty-five thousand dollar policy on the life of James Gillespie and it's still in force. The beneficiary of this policy—under a special ruling of the company—is to be selected by the executor of the last will and testament of James Gillespie, and according to instructions contained in the deceased's will."

"The Devil!" frowned Crole. "There's no telling who the beneficiary will be. He's to be picked by the executor. This insurance angle isn't of much help. Well, maybe Esther will have a report that will throw some new light on things. If it doesn't I'll have to switch to the technique of the old-time harness bulls. Grab the nearest man and beat or sweat the truth out of him." He picked up the telephone receiver and gave the operator the Police Headquarters number. "Hello," he said. "Connect me with Captain Jorgens." After a long pause the voice of Jorgens boomed over the wire.

"Hello! Who? I can't hear you."

"The name is Crole. C as in cash. R as in Rubles. O as in onions . . ."

"What is this—a class in spelling? Sorry, Crole. I'm busy whether you realize it or not. You must think that all I've got to do is listen to the lies of a notorious private dick . . ."

"Don't hang up, Captain, or you'll be sorry."

"Sorry?" The wire almost smoked before the captain's oath-crusted vocabulary ran out. "Call me next week. Do you hear? Next year!"

"I want," said Simon Crole, unabashed, "to talk to you now."

"Always you want to talk. I should think you'd get sick at the sound of your own blabberings. Well, maybe you're now going to confess . . ."

"What a one-track mind you've got, Captain. Can't you forget about me long enough to put your mind on something else?"

"On what, for instance?"

"Two men who were at the morgue yesterday looking at the body of James Gillespie. They told the attendant they represented the Guardian Life of New York. They lied. I checked with the Guardian people over long-distance telephone today. If you want a description of them, talk with your attendant."

There was a ripping sound at Jorgens' end of the wire as if the captain was tearing out his hair. A short silence, then: "You wouldn't know who these men were, would you, Simon?"

"Honestly, no. But I have a strong hunch that they're closely connected with Gillespie's death—if not the actual killers."

"Going to be in your office this evening?"

"Nope. I'm taking a lady to dinner."

"Where?"

"Wild Oaks Tavern."

"Okay, just so long as I know where I can lay hands on you." The connection clicked. Jorgens had hung up.

Crole got out his watch and looked at it. Quarter to five. Two hours yet before he had to call for Esther. He went to the window and stared intently below. In a recessed doorway across the street he saw one of Minifie's investigators.

"Taking no chances," thought the agency man. "And Jorgens no doubt has one of his own detectives watching also. Suppose I'll have to put up with being followed, but I don't like it."

He sat very quiet for a few minutes, thinking, then picked up the phone and called the Commodore. "Mr. Anderson," he directed the hotel operator.

There followed a click as the room was plugged in. A long wait, then a very faint second click. This second click was caused by the receiver in Anderson's room being taken from the hook. Yet nobody answered. He listened intently. A puzzled frown creased his forehead. Finally he spoke in an impatient undertone. "Oh the Devil, he doesn't answer." He waited for a moment, smiled knowingly at another faint click, and hung up.

Someone, he knew, was in Ned Anderson's room— someone who did not care to speak into the phone. He lifted the receiver again and called a number. "Is Scavillo and his cab in the rank? Swell. Send him down to my office, pronto. Simon Crole. Tell him I'm in one big yank."

He got up, crushed a felt hat to his head, locked up and took the elevator to the street. On the curbing in front of the building he took time out to roll a cigarette while he looked around.

The District Attorney's man had wandered absently to the same side as Crole and had taken up a position close to a Yellow cab. Crole pretended not to see him. It didn't make much difference anyhow. When it became necessary to get rid of the man, he had a system that always worked.

A few minutes later, Scavillo's cab warped to the curb and the private detective got in. Not until they had covered two blocks did the hacker turn part way around in his seat.

"Everything all right, Mr. Crole?"

"Fine, Scavillo. I'll be going to the Commodore. You're to wait for me outside. Won't be gone more than half an hour."

The driver nodded. "Did you know we were being tailed?"

"Yeah. Man from the District Attorney's office."

"Want me to pry him loose?"

"Nope. Let him ride around. He'll feel better if he knows what I'm doing and where I am."

He left the cab at a side entrance, strolled into the lobby and stopped momentarily at the desk. The clerk behind it turned stony eyes on the agency man.

"Customs inspector," lied Crole, with easy assurance, giving the clerk a momentary glance at his private detective badge. "Looking for a man named Ned Anderson. I believe he's registered here."

"Six-O-Nine," intoned the clerk. "Elevator to the right. Can we be of assistance?"

Crole wagged his head. "Think not. Routine investigation."

He got into the elevator, left it at the sixth floor and walked softly down a carpeted hall to room 609. A glance up and down the corridor. It was empty. His fingers closed around the knob. It wouldn't turn. He backed away, then came towards the door again making considerable noise.

Loudly he rapped. Waited and listened. He rapped again, shrugged and said: "Telegram for Mr. Ned Anderson."

There was movement behind the door as if someone had brushed against it. A voice said: "Slip it under the door."

"Against the rules. It's a collect telegram."

There was furtive movement beyond the door, and the slight metallic scratch as something brushed the door handle. Slowly the latch controlled by the knob began to slide back.

Crole braced himself, his big shoulder within an inch of the panel, his eyes on the knob. When he saw it turn once around he heaved forward.

The door rocketed inward, struck against a human body and sent it sprawling in an enraged heap. A thin curse blued the air. Crole kept right on moving till he was inside the room. Then closed the door behind him with a backward thrust of his heel.

The man who had fallen to the floor was scrambling to his feet. His nose looked crooked on a face that Crole was already familiar with. Here was one of the men who had visited the morgue.

"Freeze!" croaked a voice off to the right.

CHAPTER X

SLEEPING DEATH

AS IF SUDDENLY TURNED into marble, Simon Crole froze to immobility. Only his eyes refused to obey the clipped command. They pivoted in their sockets in a searching arc and focused on a small, thin man with a boyish face standing rigidly at the foot of a bed, his right arm bent sharply at the elbow, his fingers gripping a dull-blue automatic.

On this bed sprawled Ned Anderson, still clad in a dress suit, his hair tousled, his necktie askew, and an expression of mild alarm on his dark, dissolute young face.

"Simon," he said. "You shouldn't have come. These men don't want you to interrupt their efforts on my behalf. They think they can cure me of drinking. Maybe they can. But I don't want to be cured. I want to get tight and stay that way. I'd offer you a drink, but they put a sleeping powder in my last bottle."

The man who had fallen to the floor as the door crashed against him had meanwhile regained his feet and was rubbing his bruised nose with the palm of his hand. He was a big man, Crole noticed, as big as himself, and his eyes were like two chunks of smoky agate.

"Sorry," said Crole, "to have busted your nose. But it was in the way—and you with it."

"Sorry, hey?" growled Selingo, licking his thick lips. "Mister," and there was a menacing threat in his voice, "you don't know how sorry you're really gonna be."

He reached into a holster harness strapped beneath his armpit and lifted out a flat automatic—a twin to the one held so rigid by Ghost Mokund. He jammed the barrel against the ribs of the agency man.

"What's the idea of crowding in where you wasn't asked, hey? And I fell for that old wheeze of the collect telegram when I know damn well the hotel pays for all wires that come in for guests. You the guy who phoned?"

"Yeah," said Crole. "I called this room and heard somebody take the receiver from the hook. So I knew the room wasn't empty."

"Smart fella, hey? They told me where I came from that the cops in this town are easy to get along with."

"You shouldn't believe everything people tell you," reproved Crole, mildly. "The cops are plenty tough in this town—especially with hoods like you and your friend with the gat."

"So," exhaled Selingo, noisily, "you're a cop, hey? And you figure maybe to get tough . . ." His arm bent suddenly at the wrist. The automatic in his hand lashed swiftly, cruelly. The sharp edge of its gunsight raked the agency man's cheek.

Simon Crole's mildness vanished. His eyes slitted. Though big, he was fast. With a pantherish lunge he moved to the left side of Selingo so that the gunman's body was between him and Mokund's line of fire, crooked his arm in the same swift movement, and drove it upward.

His knotted fist thudded with a pile-driver smash just underneath the big gunman's ear. He followed the first blow with a looping left jab that was timed to meet Selingo's jaw as the gangster spun around.

Selingo staggered, bellowed with choking rage, and chopped viciously at Crole's face. The agency man faded backward. The automatic exploded with muffled thunder, and a bullet went into the ceiling.

The agency man straightened. His arm whipped back, then forward, gathered speed, and bunched knuckles exploded beneath Selingo's jaw. As the gunman fell, Crole kicked the automatic from his fingers. It skidded across the room, struck the leg of a heavy chair and started to spin. When it stopped its spinning, it had moved out of sight beneath the chair.

Crole lunged towards the chair, his mind intent on getting his hands on the gun. Ghost Mokund watched him with cold eyes. Took three forward steps and brought the barrel of his automatic down hard on the agency man's head.

Lights flashed across the retinas of Crole's eyes. He felt sudden pain, then the sensation of falling through breathless space where everything was shadowy and obscure.

He seemed to fall quite a distance without hitting bottom. Presently he was no longer falling, but sitting, with his back to the chair, his thoughts jumbled and unpleasant.

Ned Anderson came out of the bathroom carrying a dripping bath towel. He placed it on the agency man's head. "You're doing fine, Simon. I thought for a time that . . ."

Crole took the towel and massaged his head. "It takes more than a rap with a gun to kill me. My head's tough. Geez, but it hurts." His eyes clouded as he looked around.

Anderson interpreted the glance. "They're gone."

"How long?"

"Five minutes, maybe ten."

A ponderous sigh puffed out Crole's lips. "Too bad. And two interesting gentlemen. I talked with the police about them not more than half an hour ago. Then I meet them face to face. You didn't by any chance hear them use any names?"

"They didn't talk much except the big fellow."

By this time Crole was on his feet and reaching for a bottle of Scotch on a nearby table.

Anderson grabbed him by the arm. "Not unless you want to take a long, drugged sleep and lose your taste for liquor," he said. "I saw them put in little white sticks. The big fellow said: 'You drink this sleeping powder. It won't hurt you. It's painless. And when you wake up your taste for alcohol will be gone.' That's what he said."

Crole sniffed uneasily at the contents of the bottle. An odor, similar to that of bitter almonds, impinged upon his nostrils. "You sure as hell *would* lose your taste for alcohol if you drank this stuff," he said quietly. "For it would kill you about as quick as anything you could pour inside you. These little white sticks you saw were Cyanide of potassium. Once this chemical comes in contact with the stomach acid, it turns into Prussic acid. Its action is fast. Death in only a few minutes even with so little as one tenth of a gram. Sleeping powder? Sleeping death!"

Ned Anderson sat down abruptly. His face was white. He ran fingers through his tousled hair. "I'm glad you came, Simon."

"What did they want?"

"I already told you," said Anderson, bowing his head in the palms of his hands. "They came in, quiet like, dropped the little white sticks in the Scotch bottle, told me it wouldn't hurt to drink the stuff. Said it was necessary that I take a long sleep so that I'd forget my steady drinking."

Crole went to the bathroom, found some adhesive tape and fastened a narrow strip over the cut in his cheek. Coming back into the room he said: "You didn't drink any, did you? But of course you didn't. Otherwise, you'd still be on the bed."

"I was half-crocked, and the idea of ridding myself of the liquor habit was tempting. My future didn't look any too bright. I never was any use to anybody. Never pretended to be. Just a waster. Miss Laird sort of snapped me out of it, but it didn't last. I'm a no-good bum, fit only for the gutter."

"Please don't start crying," said Crole. "Didn't I tell you to leave everything to Simon? I meant it, too. And on a hunch that you might need a little moral courage I called you up to ask you out to supper tonight."

"I heard the bell ring. But when I started to get up the big fellow took down the receiver and the little guy pointed a gun at me. Didn't say a word, just looked at me with his fishy eyes."

"Your death was planned to look like suicide. Gunfire in a hotel is dangerous, even if the walls are thick and practically soundproof. So pack your bags," he ordered. "You're leaving."

"Leaving? Where to? I like this hotel. Why should I leave?"

"You come with me, or you stay here and get murdered."

Anderson moistened his lips. "You mean—they'll come back?"

"Don't talk," snapped the agency man. "Do like I tell you. I'm charging you a considerable fee for my agency services, Anderson. And from the looks of things, I'm going to earn every nickel of it. Take my word for it, somebody wants you out of the way. Coming to your room as they did may seem somewhat crude, but it might have worked if I hadn't blundered in when I did."

"Who would want to kill me?"

"Does it matter? Isn't the fact ugly enough? Two hundred thousand dollars is worth any kind of a risk, and believe me, these men will make another attempt unless . . ."

"Unless what?"

"Unless you get out. Leave the hotel. Take up quarters where they can't trace you. And that's my job—to protect you until I can discover who is behind all this."

"Then I'm to leave . . ."

"Now. Within five minutes."

In slightly more than five minutes everything Ned Anderson had in the room had been jammed into trunks and two bags, and the trunks were marked for the hotel storage room. Then the two men went down to the desk. Anderson paid his bill, left instructions concerning his trunks, and, with Simon Crole holding tightly to his arm he was guided through the lobby to the same entrance Crole had used in coming to the hotel.

Scavallo's cab was not in sight. Crole relinquished his hold on Anderson's arm and went out to the curb. Traffic at this time of day was dense. A stream of bright yellow cabs were jammed along the curb. For several minutes he looked up and down the street, then went back to where he had left his client.

Anderson was nowhere in sight.

Back into the hotel went the agency man, his jaw twitching. He wasn't worried—merely peeved. Downstairs he went to the cocktail bar. Anderson was seated on a red leather stool at the rail, his fingers curved around a whiskey glass.

Crole unhooked the fingers from the glass, shoved it along the bar, dropped a half dollar beside it and said to the barman: "He don't need it. Drink it yourself." Then to his client: "Next time you pull a stunt like that I'm going to smack you down. I mean it. Do you think I enjoy this business of being slapped around trying to keep you out of trouble?"

Anderson smiled crookedly. "I was thirsty."

Simon Crole lowered his voice. "Listen, Anderson. Do you remember the man who tried to kidnap Miss Laird? Well, he was murdered within a dozen feet of my office. I almost landed in jail when the killing was investigated. I still am not certain but what the District Attorney will do his damnedest to fasten that killing on me."

The eyes of Ned Anderson became serious. "But surely, Simon, they can't accuse you of a thing like that."

"They can do anything they want to, providing they can get away with it. I managed, for the time being, to beat the rap. But that doesn't mean that I can continue to. I'm not infallible. See that gray sedan parked in a 'no parking' zone, the car near the corner? There's a District Attorney investigator in that car. He's following me wherever I go."

He indicated the stream of traffic flowing beyond the curb. "And those two men who tried to poison you. Any one of these cars may be theirs. Somebody is desperately determined to destroy either one or the both of us. That's why I'm taking you away. I can take care of myself—but you . . . you're causing me quite a headache. So I'm going to sink you out of sight. Ah! There's our cab. Stick close to me," he finished, shouldering across the sidewalk and out into the street. The cab door opened. Crole shoved Anderson inside and climbed in after him. "Home, Scavillo," he called to the hacker. "And there's a gray sedan going to be tailing us. Get rid of it."

Scavillo's cab purred down the street and stopped abruptly at the first intersection where the blue light gave him the right to proceed. He waited until the last moment, just as it was turning to red, then eased the car across the street while drivers of machines moving the opposite direction had to slam on their brakes to avoid a crash. But the maneuver had placed a swarm of cars between Scavillo's cab and the pursuing machine.

At the next corner he turned right then left went through a tunnel, crossed another teeming intersection, and, once more in the clear, said from the side of his mouth: "How am I doing?"

Crole looked back. The gray sedan was no longer behind them. "All right to go home," he called.

They left the cab in front of the apartment house and went swiftly inside. At the switchboard Crole stopped. "If anyone calls or comes to ask questions about this man who's with me, just forget you saw him. As far as you're concerned, I was alone when I came in."

The girl operator, while accustomed to Simon Crole's more or less erratic behavior, looked uneasy.

"Don't worry, darling," grinned Crole. "The police aren't after him if that's what's troubling you. It's just that he's a client of mine and in need of protection."

In the quiet of the apartment Crole looked at his watch. "Haven't much time if we're to pick up Esther by seven. And by God! If anything happens to keep me from eating tonight, I'll go stark insane. Step on it, Anderson. Get your clothes changed. This spot is gonna be your home for a time."

At five minutes to seven Crole, bathed, shaved and dressed in evening clothes, looked through a parted curtain to the street outside. Scavillo had returned and his cab was at the curb. Anderson came to the big detective's side. He was white, shaky.

"You think it's going to be all right—my going out to dinner?"

"Sure. The place where we're going is almost like a private home. Nobody'll bother us there. All set. Let's go."

The Wild Oaks Tavern was once a wealthy man's home. The wealthy man had sold it. Remodeled, it became a landmark of respectability. Hidden in the foothills at the extreme north boundary of the coastal city, far off the main boulevard, it was a retreat men and women could not enter unless they knew of its existence and were admitted by a husky doorman who knew all its regular patrons.

A rambling structure of gabled roofs, dormers, and odd-shaped private rooms, it was the rendezvous of oil men, wealthy ranchers, screen stars and gourmets.

The doorman did not unbend from his loftiness when he saw Crole and his party. He looked at Anderson, then questioningly at the private detective.

"Friend of mine," said Crole. "He's quite all right."

"And the lady?"

"An old friend of mine. She's been here before."

"Very good. Step inside. The lounge is on the right."

It wasn't until they were seated at a table in a private room that Simon Crole felt he could relax. "Well," he sighed. "I feel very old tonight. Esther, you look beautiful in that emerald green dress. If you should wear that gown in court, you'd knock the jurymen cold."

A waiter came in bearing gifts in the form of cocktails.

Esther Manning sipped her sidecar with enjoyment. She was tall, slender and strikingly beautiful. From a department store detective she had gravitated to Crole's agency and had been a clever operator. Police and social service work had taken her from him. Then the law had called. Now she was a member of the bar, serene, competent and still ambitious. She smiled fondly at the big, round-faced man with the bald head.

"You knew, Simon, that Ned and I were old friends?"

"That's the first thing I told him," said Anderson.

"Yes," said Crole, savoring his old-fashioned. "I knew that. And it made me feel sad. That former friendship kept me from earning a fee of twenty thousand dollars. I hope, some-day, that I'll be able to forget that huge fee. Right now it rankles inside me like a twinge of rheumatism."

The waiter came in with food.

"Double order of everything for me," said Crole, unfolding a napkin and taking a firm grip on the silver.

The meal was leisurely and quiet. Over demitasse Crole said: "I'm a mild, patient man, Esther. But my patience is at an end now that my bodily needs have temporarily been as-suaged. What did you find out?"

Esther Manning picked up a spoon and traced an invisible pattern on the table cloth. "Mr. Anderson's house in Los Gatos canyon was sold for eighteen thousand dollars cash to a man by the name of Henry Brenan of London . . ."

"Henry Brenan, Henry Brenan," repeated Crole. "You sure that's the man's name who bought it?"

"I've still got a good memory, Simon."

"A lot better than mine. Ummm!"

"Why did you ask?"

"Nothing," said Crole, thinking of the oblong of cardboard that looked as if it might have at one time been fastened to a key. If the cardboard had been fastened to the key with a piece of string, then somebody must have recently decided to make use of the key and had torn off the string and card-board. Could Gillespie have done this? Or had Coughlin been sent to the office for the key?

The orchestra started to play softly. Esther became restless. Anderson rose gallantly. "May I?" he offered.

"I'll be back, Simon," promised the girl.

Alone, but far from lonesome, Simon Crole leaned farther back in the chair, crossed his big hands over his chest, and allowed his eyes to droop shut.

His thoughts began to arouse vague questionings now that he was contented and well-fed. He could forget about the house in Los Gatos canyon. Legally, it was out of reach and the owner in London. That left George Baron who had of-fered him a big sum to bring back a fugitive witness from the east, and the two men who had attempted to poison Anderson.

But wait a minute. That wasn't all. There was still Edward Smith from Lima, Ohio. What was it Coughlin had whispered? Gillespie's double. But why double? Was it that Smith resembled Gillespie? Suppose he did? Maybe it was important. But why?

The big detective opened his eyes long enough to roll a cigarette, pour himself a drink, then began to brood about Coughlin. If the other private detective had had a secret file, where the devil did he have it? In his office, undoubtedly. He speculated on the possibility of burglary.

Esther and Anderson came back, flushed, happy. "Gorgeous music, Simon. Want to . . ."

Crole had risen. "An old buzzard like me dance with a charming girl like you? Perish the thought, darling. I know my good points, and dancing isn't among them."

Anderson poured himself a drink from Crole's bottle. "This is a grand place, Simon. This liquor all right to drink?"

"Has been right along, and I'm still awake."

"I'm not a drunk, Simon. I'm just a victim of the stuff." He sat back, smiled pleasantly, and began to hum quietly that sad, minor lamentation expressing a gnawing sorrow.

Esther said, as Crole held a match to her cigarette: "Why so pensive this evening, Simon? Everything all right?"

"Nothing's ever all right. If it isn't one thing it's another. I almost had a murder rap pinned on me this afternoon. If I had any hair, I'm sure it would have turned white within the hour."

"Murder rap?"

"Yes. An agency man named Coughlin. Mortally wounded, he staggered into my office and practically died in my arms."

"Was he able to tell you who . . .?"

"He thought he was telling me, but I couldn't hear what he gasped. There was plenty of confusion in the old office for a while. The D.A. thinks I'm implicated. Captain Jorgens can't make up his mind. Meanwhile there's a man named Edward Smith who fits in somewhere. I'm trying to trace him. Matt's

gone by plane to Lima, Ohio, to check from that point west-
ward."

"You mentioned earlier an offer of twenty thousand dollars," said Esther. "Who's behind it?"

"A man named George Baron."

"The attorney?"

"Know him?"

Esther examined her pink finger nails. "Yes, and I think
he's one of the most handsome, debonair gentlemen I have
ever met. A slick, conscienceless man who knows always
what he wants, and how to obtain it with the minimum of
effort."

"It makes me feel ill," admitted Crole, ruefully, "to have
had to turn down his offer. I could have handled it through a
New York agency, but he would have none of it. He wanted
me to take it personally. Since I was already hooked up with
Anderson, I had to let it go by the boards. Twenty thousand
dollars," he mused. "Any way you look at it, Esther, that's
considerable money these days."

The waiter knocked discreetly on the door and came in
holding a telephone in his hands. He plugged the loose end
of the cord into a socket close to the table, looked at Crole,
said: "The gentleman said it was very important. Otherwise I
wouldn't have bothered you."

"Okay," said Crole, squinting doubtfully at the instrument.
He knew who that call would be from. Only one man knew
where he was.

After the waiter had gone Esther asked. "Who is it?"

"The police," sighed Crole.

He took the receiver from the hook. "Simon Crole speaking. Oh! Good evening, Captain. Ummm! You would have
something of a disagreeable nature to discuss. All right. I'll
wait. Why should I run away? Where could I go? Now listen.
This place where I am is respectable. So if you've got a lot
of cops with you, park them outside. Okay. Bye."

Esther spoke casually. "You seem to be in some difficulty
with the police."

"That isn't unusual. Captain Jorgens is compelled to play along with the District Attorney's office. At the same time, if there is a pinch to be made, he wants his office to get the full credit. It isn't anything I hold against him. It's just that we're two different men. But we manage to get along—after a fashion."

He rubbed his hands briskly. "One thing more, Esther, I want you to do for me, and I'll swear it will be the last. If you have Henry Brenan's address in London. I wish you'd telephone London and verify the sale of the house. Have you any connections there?"

Esther nodded. "David Spindler, a wholesale jeweler. He'll do anything I ask him to."

"Swell. And the house is vacant now, I suppose?"

"Except for a caretaker, a Mexican and his family."

"Well, now that that's off my mind . . . Oh, oh! Do you hear the same thing I do?"

Faintly as though far away came the moaning of a siren.

Esther crossed her silken-clad knees, lighted a cigarette, smiled with pleasurable excitement, and said: "It's your party, Simon. But I hope it isn't a pinch."

"So do I," sighed Crole. "But whatever happens, the captain can't take away my appetite with his dark hints and outright insinuations. I'm comfortable and well fed. The evening is still young. And with one more drink I'll be in full possession of all my faculties."

He reached for the bottle of rye. But a disturbance in the corridor stayed his hand. He shrugged helplessly, leaned back and waited for the inevitable—his friendly enemy, Captain Jorgens.

CHAPTER XI

BEHIND THE PICTURE

DISTRESSED AND SLIGHTLY APOLOGETIC, the waiter opened the door. Crole smiled benignly. "We're expecting him," he said. "Show the Captain in and see that we're not disturbed."

Captain Jorgens, bulky, grim and black-mustached, stood framed in the doorway staring into the private room. His jaundiced eyes of suspicion swerved from one face to another as if he expected to read guilt in all of them.

From somewhere he produced a half-hearted attempt at something intended for a smile at sight of Esther Manning. Crole he merely favored with a bleak glance. Anderson he didn't know and showed no hesitation in saying so. "Who's this man?"

Crole got up. "Ned," he said. "Meet the best and most suspicious police officer on the coastal city force. Captain, this gentleman is my client, Mr. Ned Anderson. Will the Captain join my little party and accept a drink?"

"No," frowned Jorgens. "I'm on duty—and here on business."

"Right, quite right," said Crole, unperturbed by the other's gruffness. "Duty is always something to be treated with respect. I admire your attitude, Captain, but I distrust your thirst."

He filled two glasses with rye, took one himself and extended the other towards the scowling police officer. Jorgens twisted stubby fingers around the glass, drank the rye at a single swallow, blinked and frowned as he returned the glass to the table.

"Simon," he began. "I think it is about time for you to explain what you know about James Gillespie's secretary, a

young lady by the name of Virginia Laird. I've been searching the city for her, quietly so as not to arouse too much suspicion, but she can't be found. It looks as though she might
be able to throw considerable light on things. She may even
be an accessory . . ."

Anderson shuddered and started up in his chair.

"Easy, Ned," soothed Crole, placing a restraining hand on
his client's shoulder.

Jorgens said exultingly: "Looks as though I rang the bell."

Crole leaned back in his chair. "If you did, I didn't hear it."
He grinned pleasantly.

"You know her then?"

"Yes," agreed Crole, as if knowing her meant absolutely
nothing. "We know her. And I suppose that at this moment
Virginia Laird is somewhere east of Kansas . . . Anderson,
have you got that wire Miss Laird sent from Kansas City?"

Anderson pawed at his pocket. "The wire," he said, "was
sent to Miss Laird's mother. She has it, or had. All I've got is
this unfinished note she wrote to me."

He took a folded sheet of paper from his pocket—the one
Crole had found in her desk, and extended it to the police
captain.

Jorgens read the typed words, chewed thoughtfully on his
lower lip and looked up sharply at Anderson. "When did you
receive this?"

"We found it," said Crole. "Or rather I did, in the girl's
desk yesterday around noontime. I was sort of looking the
place over, as it were."

"What do you mean—as it were? You know damned well
you were giving the place a thorough going over since nobody was there to stop you. Someday, Simon, you're going
to run up against a police officer who isn't as tolerant as I
am. And when you do, it's just going to be too bad for you."
He cleared his throat with a harsh rattle and snapped at
Anderson: "What about this telegram? This is the first I've
heard about it."

Anderson looked startled. "No, nothing special, Captain. It
looked all right to me."

"What did it say?"

"I don't remember the exact words. Something like this: Don't worry. Going to New York on business. Love. Virginia."

Jorgens grunted.

"You can check on that, Captain," said Crole, "by taking a ride out to where Miss Laird lives with her mother. And that will dispose of Miss Laird for the present."

"Think so?"

"I don't see why not."

"Who sent her east in the first place? Where, exactly, did she go? And for what reason?"

"I suppose her employer."

"He's dead."

"But he could have sent her before he died, couldn't he?"

"Possibly, but did he, Simon?"

"I wouldn't know, Captain. But if you're trying to prove her an accessory before the fact, you're all wet."

"You keep out of this, Simon. I'm going to ask Anderson a few questions. There's something being kept back, and I'm going to get to the bottom of this case, or . . ."

"Anderson's my client," said Crole. "He don't have to answer your questions, Jorgens—at least not now. But," he raised his hand, palm outward, "I'll be glad to do so in my own way."

"Maybe you're this man's mouthpiece . . ."

"Miss Manning's his attorney, if that's what you mean. I'm simply—sort of a spiritual adviser."

"Mr. Crole is well within his rights," said Esther, speaking for the first time. "The legal aspects . . ."

"Phooey!" spat Jorgens. "Aspects be damned. What I want is a little information, not a lecture from a couple of crime sharks."

"Tsk, tsk!" clucked Crole. "You're sore, Captain, or you wouldn't make such nasty remarks. What's the difference who answers your questions?"

"Knowing you as I do, Simon, I would say, conservatively, that the difference would be considerable. You have a way of stripping the truth of the essentials and giving me what's left over."

"You wouldn't have felt that way if I had gone to the D.A's. office and put them on the right track in regard to Gillespie being murdered. I gave you that choice piece of information and you profited by it. But I'm wasting your time, and God knows, you're spoiling a quiet party of mine."

Captain Jorgens relaxed from his stiff attitude. "Another rye, Simon. We'd better stop fighting before we kill each other. Now tell me," he said, reaching for the amber-colored glass, "where your client, also Miss Manning, fits into the picture."

Crole told him, swiftly, and sparsely of certain details, how Anderson had arrived in California. How he had been met on the first night by Miss Laird, of her fears and suspicions. Of Ned's subsequent investigation of his bank account—omitting any reference to the house in Los Gatos canyon, and what he had lately discovered. He did mention, however, the attempted kidnapping.

"It looks," observed Jorgens, when the agency man had finished, "as if your estate, Anderson, has passed beyond the bounds of recovery. Gillespie's murder was undoubtedly motivated by the two hundred thousand dollars he withdrew from the bank sometime before your arrival. It also explains the open safe and the absence of a number of stocks and bonds that belonged to other customers."

"I'm afraid I'm a poor man," shrugged Anderson.

"Ummmm!" grunted Jorgens. "Afraid? Gillespie got your money all right. That's perfectly obvious. And somebody took it away from Gillespie. You're broke, and who the hell's to pay Simon Crole his fee? By cripes, Simon," chuckled Jorgens. "Excuse me for laughing in your face. No money, no fee. It's gonna break your heart."

He got up laughing. "Bye," he called from the doorway. "Be seeing you, Simon." He was still laughing as he closed the door and moved down the corridor.

Simon Crole smiled bemusedly. "I wouldn't have believed it, Esther, if I hadn't heard it with my own ears. Never, as long as I've known him, have I heard Captain Jorgens laugh."

"It's a funny world," Anderson observed. "Only it's my money that's been stolen. And it seems only right that if anybody got a laugh out of it, I should be the one. But I can't laugh. I get sick just thinking about all those dollars of mine in a bank under somebody else's name."

Simon Crole's voice was grave. "Didn't I tell you, Ned, to leave everything to me, that you would soon be wealthy again?"

"That's what you told me. But I'm beginning to weaken."

"There are angles to this case, Ned, that Captain Jorgens isn't aware of, and which, naturally enough, I have not acquainted him with. You may recall, if you're sober enough, his remark about my way of stripping the truth of the essentials and giving him what's left over. And that's exactly what I did. I gave him what I had left over, and reserved the choice parts for myself since I am inherently a selfish person and devoted to the rights of my clients who pay me fees. Does that sound involved?"

"It does," remarked Esther. "Simon, you should have been a lawyer."

"Jorgens once remarked I should have been a horse thief."

"Get me my money back," said Anderson, "and my house—don't overlook the house, I'm sentimental about that old shack. Twenty-one rooms. You do this, Simon, and like I said, I'll double the amount you were offered to leave this city and abandon my case."

"I wouldn't think of leaving town, Ned," said Crole. "But I do think it's time we were going home. Ned's staying with me, Esther. Two hoods got into his hotel room and tried to bump him off. I'm afraid to leave him where they can find him. Figured my place was not known to them, and he'd be safe for—until I trip them two hoods up and pin a murder rap on them."

"It's awful early to be leaving," said Esther, "but you know what you're doing I suppose. By the way, did a Mexican named José Hernandez come to your office?"

Crole nodded. "Yes. About his kid, Manuel. I sent Matt out to his place to throw a scare into the lad. You remarked about a Mexican caretaker on Anderson's old homestead on Los Gatos canyon. This gives me an idea. Do you think I could trust Hernandez to find out a few things from that caretaker?"

Esther nodded. "José probably knows every Mexican in the county, and is highly respected by all of them. And he's a clever man."

"I'll look him up in the morning," finished Crole. "Shall we go now?"

Simon Crole left the taxi and went with Esther as far as her front door. Here he paused and said: "You won't forget the telephone call to London. Make it as early as possible. I'll pay the charges both ways. And ring my office the moment you get a report."

"I didn't hear you say anything about paying me," said the girl.

"I'm not supposed to pay you. But if you see some pretty bauble in one of the nice stores and like it—why, have it charged to Simon. And don't go over two dollars."

"The bauble I'm likely to pick out will cost more than two dollars, you skinflint. Two hundred is what you'll have to pay."

Crole patted her shoulder. "The sky's the limit, girl. You know that. Bye."

As the taxi approached his apartment house, Simon Crole leaned close to the window and peered searchingly along the sidewalks. At first glance they seemed deserted. But he was not deceived. Across from the apartment house entrance was a Monterey cypress tree. And lounging in its deep shadows was the dim figure of a man. Somebody was watching his apartment, waiting for him to return.

"Changed my mind," said Crole to the hacker.

"Keep right on going. Not too fast, and turn right on the next corner."

He turned to Anderson. "Man watching my place, I think. Can't take the risk. I guess it means another hotel. Driver, take us to the Franklin Hotel on San Felice Boulevard."

Anderson shrugged and was quiet during the cross-town trip. At the hotel both men got out and Crole dismissed the cab. He went to the desk with his client. Saw him registered and in his room. Then turned to go. "You'll find this a quiet place, Ned. My advice is to have your meals in the room. Keep in touch with me at my office by telephone."

Anderson shrugged moodily. "I've been thinking, Simon. Could Miss Laird's trip east have any connection with the offer that was made to you?"

"That's a smart thought, Anderson, but I'm glad you made no mention of it in front of Jorgens. It would have complicated things more than they are now. Forget it. And stick close to this room. And do not, under any condition, leave it without direct word from me or my office. As long as you're in danger, you must keep off the streets if you want to live. After what happened this evening, you ought to realize that these people mean business."

"I do," nodded Anderson. "And I'm still scared—been scared witless all evening. Everything's in your hands. I'm trusting you absolutely."

"Swell." Crole's face twisted into its perpetual surprised smile. "Be seeing you. And remember, don't leave the room. Got plenty of money?"

"I cashed a check this afternoon. Yes, I've got plenty. Need any more fee payments?"

"I'm not as bad as Captain Jorgens makes me out to be. Whatever my client pays me, I earn. In fact I leave it entirely to their judgment. No, you keep your money for your own needs. And don't do anything without an order from me."

"Right," said Anderson. "But there's nothing to stop me from . . . ?"

"From taking a few drinks?" finished Crole. "Not the slightest. I know you can hold it. Act the gentleman and keep your head."

"I'd feel better, Simon, if Gillespie hadn't been murdered."

"Don't let a little thing like that bother you, Ned. Gillespie isn't dead."

"Eh? Not dead? Then I'm the one that's dead. Good Lord, Simon, didn't I hear you tell Jorgens that you pointed out the fact that his death wasn't an accident, but deliberate murder? And didn't I read all the horrible details in the papers?"

"Quite so, Ned. I let loose a piece of information because I could no longer use it. I thought it would keep Jorgens out of my hair. Coughlin's death caused me many uneasy moments, but one fact still stands out. Gillespie is alive."

Ned Anderson's eyes bugged out. "What makes you think so?"

"Veteran instincts, Ned, and a knowledge of crime, how it happens and why. I call it a hunch. But I've got my hooks out and they're bound to snag on something before the next twenty-four hours. Meanwhile, I must get back to my apartment and make the acquaintance of the gentleman who is waiting for me across the street."

He pivoted, left the room and went out to the street. It took a few minutes to find a cab. Finally he located one and was driven to his apartment.

He didn't get out directly in front, but a few doors beyond. Humming, he stood for a moment staring at nothing in particular, then crossed over to the other side of the street.

The man he had seen earlier was still at his post in the deep shadows. Crole stopped humming and accosted him. "Looking for somebody, Mister?"

"What's it to you?"

"Nothing, particularly. Perhaps I'm the man you've been waiting so long for. My name's Simon Crole. Does that convey anything to you? If it doesn't, okay. If it does—I'd suggest you come up to my apartment and have a drink. Nothing like a nightcap of Scotch or rye to ease off—er, difficulties of a doubtful nature."

"So you're Simon Crole, eh?" said the man stepping out to the sidewalk.

Crole's face showed no trace of the disappointment he felt. The man before him in the soft light of the street lights was neither of the two men he had earlier encountered in Anderson's room. "Yeah, I'm Simon Crole. And who the devil are you?"

"Me? Don't be in such a rush. I'll talk—at the right time. Been wanting to talk for hours. That's why I've been hanging around, waiting for you to come home. Damn right I'll talk, plenty. How about that drink you mentioned?"

"The drink. Of course. But we'd better move inside. I don't like the night air. And I want to sit down where I'll be comfortable." He turned and led the way into his apartment building.

Stopping at the switchboard he smiled at the girl. "Anybody call or leave any phone numbers to call?"

"Nobody's been here, Mr. Crole," said the girl, her eyes on the cords plugged in the switchboard. "A man called and left his number. Do you want me to ring him?" Still her eyes didn't meet his. She handed him a small piece of paper. "Here's his number."

Crole took the paper and read it before crumpling it and dropping it back on the board: "A man from the Edison company was in your apartment while you were away."

"Thanks," said Crole. "I don't think I want to talk to him now. I'll ring him in the morning. G'night."

"Good night," said the girl, her eyes still on the cord plugs.

As Crole clicked the key into the door the man behind him said: "Some swell apartment." The door opened inward. He looked around. "You must be sitting pretty. This place has class."

Crole went from one room to the other snapping on lights. "Have a chair," he invited. "Yes, it's quite a place." But his eyes were ranging over every article of furniture in the living room. For years, while living with apparent careless abandon, he always kept his furniture in certain spots. The drapes were never disturbed. Pictures remained just so. His eyes were accustomed to them.

But tonight he sensed that something had been disturbed. The woman that took care of his apartment would never think of violating the arrangement. Yet something was definitely out of line. There was an alien something about the room that was disturbing.

He lifted the top of a radio cabinet, and a miniature bar came to view. "Scotch or Rye?" he inquired.

"Rye," said his night visitor.

Crole set a bottle of rye and two glasses on a small taboret which he moved into position between two deep-cushioned chairs. Fumbling for matches he again allowed his eyes to range over the room for the thing that disturbed him. He knew it was there. He was prepared to find it. And did.

He sighed gustily as his big frame settled into the deep-cushioned chair. But his eyes were grave with suppressed fury.

To his left, as he sat down, high on the wall, was a marine study done in oil by Frank Cuprien, a noted west-coast artist. It was a fairly large painting of the Pacific, depicting restless waves at sundown. There was no sun in the picture, only its reflection from the clouds. A restful scene of soft, luminescent upheavals of water.

But to Simon Crole, as he sighed and faced his night caller, all the charm and restfulness of the painting had vanished. In its place was a savage resentment.

During his absence the picture had been moved, tampered with, and now hung shamefully askew.

And Simon Crole, filling his visitor's glass with rye, knew, as though he had placed it there himself, what lay behind the crooked picture on the wall.

CHAPTER XII

A NEW ALLY

DISSEMBLING, CROLE SMILED across the taboret. "How's the rye?" he asked.

"Fine. Mind if I have another?"

"Help yourself."

The man helped himself, meanwhile studying the big, hard-muscled body of Simon Crole slumped lazily in the chair. Finally he spoke in a clipped voice. "I guess it's time we got down to business, Crole. What do you say?"

"I've been waiting for you to start talking. Go ahead. I'm a good listener."

"To get down to cases, Crole. I'm a private detective like yourself. I am or was a partner of Joe Coughlin."

"Didn't know Joe Coughlin had a partner."

"Nothing like being wised to a certain fact, is there?"

Crole blinked and lighted a cigarette. "The more I know about people, the safer I feel. You included. Tell me some more."

"Sure. Why not? Now listen. Joe was working in-dependently on a case which I wasn't in on. Sometimes we handle our work that way. But though he didn't tell me what it was all about, I knew he was worried. He was so worried that he wrote a note and left it on my desk."

From his pocket the man took a small square of paper. "This isn't the original, Crole. I got the real copy put away where it is safe. Want me to read what my partner wrote?"

"If you're not too ignorant."

"Forget the sarcasm. Here's what he writes: 'I am afraid I will have to drop this case I'm working on. Already I'm into something that's close to breaking a certain legal statute that carries a penalty of life imprisonment or death. Should Simon Crole interfere in my affairs, the result might turn out badly for me. For there is only one man in this city who I am afraid of—and that man is Simon Crole. I went into this case with my eyes open, but it looks, from the way things are shaping up, that I am going to be forced into something that will cause a Grand Jury investigation. I think I'll have to see Crole and have a talk with him.' How's that strike you as a piece of evidence?"

"Smack between the eyes. It's some document, and no doubt genuine. Coughlin must have been scared as hell when he wrote it."

"Yes, I think he was—and with good reason."

"All this," said Crole, "is highly instructive yet somewhat vague. Suppose we get down to hard facts. You have your reason for reading Coughlin's reflections to me. He must have had something on his conscience when he wrote it."

"He had *you* on his conscience. He was afraid of what might happen to him. He was afraid you might learn so much of his activities that you'd become panicky and kill him to close his mouth."

Crole picked up a butt from the tray and lighted it. "You're still shooting in the dark. I don't consider myself dense, but your point, in spite of what you have already disclosed, still eludes me."

"The point *is* that I haven't as yet taken this piece of evidence to the police. I thought I'd wait until I had a talk with you."

Crole inhaled deeply and allowed the smoke to dribble from nostrils and mouth in twin gray clouds. "I think I get your point. You want something from me in return for Coughlin's written words. A form of shake-down."

"You might call it that."

"Or possibly, blackmail."

"Call it anything you want to. I'm out for the dough—a big chunk. You've got plenty. So I figured that the original of what I just read to you would be worth more in your hands than—say the hands of the District Attorney for instance."

"Got it all figured out, eh?"

"Yes. And it adds up right either way."

"How much are you demanding?"

"Ten grand. Cash. In the morning."

Simon Crole exhaled noisily. "Whew! That's a lot of money. Too much. I'd like to have that piece of evidence. It would make me quite happy. But I'd never buy it from you. It isn't worth it. Besides, I never pay out blackmail. It's against my principles."

"I'm simply telling you how it is, Crole. You know damned well that you bumped off my partner. So does the D.A. This piece of evidence would provide the motive that District Attorney Minifie failed to uncover when his investigators were in your office after Joe Coughlin's murder."

Crole's ordinarily pleasant eyes began to cloud over. He said: "What's your name? I don't remember that you told me."

"I didn't. My name doesn't matter."

"Then I'll call you one. Right to your face. You're a rat—a vicious, snarling rat trying to cash in on your partner's death. There may be a form of human scum lower than you are, but I have yet to discover it."

He got up from his chair and stood towering above the other man. His eyes slitted, and unconsciously his fists knotted. He stepped back, however, as the chunky muzzle of an automatic jammed against his stomach.

"I've got a permit, Crole, to carry this gun. Make a pass at me, and I'll spill your supper all over the carpet."

Crole continued to back away, his lips twisted in their smile of surprise. Slowly he raised his hand, the left one, palm upwards and extended it towards the marine picture on the wall.

"It won't be necessary to take down the picture to see what's behind it. I know what's there without having to see it—a small microphone for trapping the human voice. There'll be wires running to an artificial diaphragm that exactly reproduces our voices on a wax phonograph record. The stylus cuts a wavy line that never lies. It was a cheap set-up and hardly worthy of a brainy man like our District Attorney."

A thin smile of admiration curled the other man's lips. "Smart, aren't you?"

"Not too smart," said Crole, wagging his bald head from side to side. "Just disappointed in the man who tried to make use of you to frame me with something so crude as black-mail."

He sat down abruptly and poured himself a drink. His voice had a cutting edge. "You can get the hell out of my apartment anytime now, and take your wires and dictaphone apparatus with you. I suspect the rest is hooked up in an ad-joining apartment. Take it and get out—before I lose my temper and kick you out."

He watched his caller rest his gun arm on a table while he lifted the receiver of the telephone and called a number.

District Attorney Minifie, red-eyed, his nerves raw from the constant bickering of news reporters, sat behind a cluttered desk in his home. There were two telephones on the desk. One was a private wire to his own office. The second was for outside calls. This second one was ringing now.

He took down the receiver. His voice reflected the deep weariness of an over-worked body. "Yes," he said.

"Leahy speaking," said a voice. "I'm at Crole's apart-ment."

A hopeful light came into the District Attorney's eyes. "Well?"

"What'll I do? The plan fizzled. I don't know why. But it did."

District Attorney Minifie picked up a pencil and placed the point against the desk blotter. In a space not already covered with other pencil markings he drew a circle. Inside the circle he drew a square. The square he divided into four right an-gles. "Get anything at all on the record?"

"Nothing but abuse."

"Hmmm! He knew about the apparatus, then?"

"As if he'd installed it himself."

The District Attorney grinned dourly. "Well, it's too bad. Convey him my apologies. I don't want him sore at me." He hung up.

Leahy pocketed his gun and said: "The D.A. says he's sorry he done you wrong, and for you not to get sore. That make you feel better?"

"There's still some rye left," said Crole. "And Leahy, who the hell's idea was this in the first place?"

"I'll take another drink," said Leahy. He poured the rye, regarded it seriously, said: "Daniels' idea. I'm the sucker who was picked to see it through since I was an unknown to you. But what I said about Coughlin was correct. We were partners in that we shared the same office, though we worked independent of each other, sharing the fees between us."

Crole clasped his hands around his knees. "I'm sorry about calling you a rat, Leahy. But I had in mind a man selling his dead partner's murderer freedom for the ten grand you mentioned."

"That's all right."

"You still running the business now that your partner is dead?"

"Sure. What else can I do?"

"Working on anything right now?"

"This little job for the D.A. He said it ought to be good for a few days more. Looks like it's washed up now."

"It is, Leahy." Crole searched for a butt, failed to find one, so was forced to roll his cigarette. When all this was attended to he found his glass empty. He filled it. He emptied it. He smacked his lips, said: "I seem to be busy as hell doing nothing in particular." He leaned back in his chair and studied the man. "How'd you like to work for me?" he asked.

Leahy toyed with his glass. His hat up to this moment had remained on his head. He took it off. His hair was sandy, thin, but well combed. He had large blue eyes and an undistinguished face. From the band of his hat he took a square of paper. He grinned as he placed it on the taboret.

"The original, Crole, of that thing I read to you."

"It doesn't mean anything to me, Leahy."

"Probably not. I'm showing you that I have it. In other words I'm laying it in your hands if you want it—for nothing."

"The hell!" grunted Crole, rising up. "A few minutes ago I would have liked that piece of paper as an interesting keepsake. It revealed a strange fact, Leahy. Coughlin was afraid of me. He shouldn't have been—unless he broke some law that might involve me."

"Don't you ever go outside the law, Crole?"

"My enemies say I do—but they've never proved it."

"Why was Joe afraid of you? But before you answer—I'll be damned glad to work for you or with you, whatever you say."

Simon Crole nodded absently. "Consider yourself hired. Now to get back to your former partner. The legal statute he referred to was an attempted kidnapping. The victim was a young woman—the secretary to the late James Gillespie. The snatch wasn't a success. A man named Anderson took the girl from her abductor. That man was a client of mine. And Coughlin knew it. And because he knew it, he was afraid that—well, you know how he felt."

"Yes, that's plenty clear."

"Another thing," Crole resumed. "I have a notion that Coughlin wanted to get clear from the people he was working for. He knew, or should have known, that he was in for trouble if he didn't. But whoever he worked for would not loosen their hold. They forced him to come to my office and borrow my gun in the name of the District Attorney."

A startled look appeared in Leahy's blue eyes. "That explains a certain telephone conversation. Hell, Crole. I remember now. It was a half or three quarters of an hour before he got bumped off that the phone in our office rang. He answered it. Someone must have been urging him to something he wasn't willing to do. He finally said that he'd see this guy and talk it over with him. Then he went out."

"And you made no effort to trace this call or sound out Coughlin?"

"Why should I? It was his case, not mine."

"Did you know, Leahy, that while this telephoning was going on I was in the District Attorney's office? He had me on the carpet on another matter that was brought about by a strange man telling him over the wire that I was no doubt responsible for Gillespie's murder. While I was out of my office Coughlin comes in and tells my secretary the District Attorney sent him after my gun."

He slapped both knees with the palms of his hands. "And I had hardly more than returned to my office when Coughlin comes weaving in, a bullet through his insides. I carried him to my couch. He was sinking fast. He tried to tell me who did it. He thought before he passed out that he *had* told me. But his whispers were too faint. He did, however, murmur something about making a snatch and failing, also something about . . ."

"About what?" asked Leahy.

"This is the delicate part," smiled Crole, "and we'll have to take each other on trust."

"My hole card is that piece of paper," said Leahy, "written by Joe." He picked it up, shredded it in small pieces, dropped it in an ash tray and set fire to the torn pieces with a match. "That's the way I feel about the whole thing, Crole. I wasn't nuts about the idea of trying to frame you, but when I read that thing to the D.A. he seemed to think there was something behind it. But it was Daniels who arranged the blackmail trap."

He got to his feet and crushed a felt hat to his head. "I don't need anything you've got, Crole. I tried to sneak over a fast one on you, and you called the deal, though how the hell you did it I don't know—or care. You've got no reason to trust me, and I'm not holding it against you."

"That being the case," Crole drawled from the deep-cushioned chair, "sit down. We'll kill what's left of the rye, then be on our way downtown."

"The rye," said Leahy, "is something I can understand. But what's downtown this time of night?"

"Your office, Leahy."

"There's nothing there, Crole . . ."

"Oh, but there is," insisted Crole. "There's something there that Joe Coughlin whispered about when he lay dying in my office. A something or other, Leahy, that Joe Coughlin called his 'Secret File.' And I'll pay you well if you'll help me obtain it."

A frown of annoyance creased Leahy's forehead. Crole sensed a checkmate. "Maybe you don't understand what it is I mean?"

"I understand all right. It was a small memorandum book with loose leaves. It was in Joe's desk when the District Attorney's men descended on the office and grabbed everything movable and took it with them for examination."

Simon Crole grinned ruefully. "Well, it's too bad. I had a hunch that I'd find the key to the solution of a couple of murders in that secret file."

Leahy's face brightened. "Maybe I can get it," he said. "They don't know themselves what it's all about. And it's possible that they haven't made out a list of what they took from the office. At least they haven't given me any kind of receipt."

For several moments Crole rubbed his bald head. The book in question, he knew, was safe in the District Attorney's office. In times past things had been taken from the prosecutor's files—things of a harmful nature that involved big men in the state.

But he, Simon Crole, was not a big man. Nor was Anderson. They were just two ordinary people. It had been on his mind earlier in the evening to attempt a small burglary by visiting Coughlin's former office and searching the records for this particular item.

Whether he would have actually gone through with his plan he did not know. He had been toying with the idea, testing its feasibility and chances of success. Meanwhile the investigators had jumped in and taken everything, and the one thing he wanted and needed was jammed in with a lot of other records in the property room of the Municipal building where Minifie had his offices.

He looked up suddenly into the blue eyes of the other man. "Leahy," he said, "I want that loose-leaf book that Coughlin called his secret file, not because there's anything in it incriminating to me, but for other reasons. And I wouldn't think of asking you to go down to the D.A.'s office and deliberately steal it. That wouldn't be ethical."

"It might be done at that," mused Leahy.

"But if such a thing could be accomplished without risk," Crole resumed, "I would be immensely pleased. So pleased, you understand, that I'd be willing to show my appreciation to the extent of five hundred dollars."

"The money," said Leahy, approvingly, "I could use to pay off the balance on a car I bought two months ago." A wide grin split his face. He extended his hand. "You've hired a new operator for a few days. I'll go down to the D.A.'s office in the morning."

Crole took the extended hand. "Fine. I like your directness, Leahy. But remember this. No man ever feared or hated me because I was on the wrong side of law and order. I play a straight game, but I don't overlook any tricks, provided I can get away with them." He sighed lugubriously. "Sorry the rye is gone. If you want some gin . . ."

"Hell with gin," said Leahy. "I'm going home and get some sleep. See you tomorrow."

After his caller had gone, Crole wandered to the front window and watched him move down the street. Then he went downstairs himself and leaned against the switchboard in the front hall.

"You're more intelligent, dear," he told the girl, "than most young ladies. Here's for the tip you passed on to me when I came in with the gentleman who just left." He extended a twenty-dollar bill.

"You're swell, Mr. Crole. Why shouldn't a girl do things for a tenant like you?"

"I wonder myself at times. But it doesn't always work out that way. Be seeing you," he added, plodding up the stairs. "G'night."

"Good night," echoed the girl.

Alone in his apartment once more, Crole switched on a table lamp and turned off the overhead lights. He removed the empty rye bottle and dropped it in a square hole in the wall. He heard it go sliding down a chute and the distant crash of broken glass as it smashed against another bottle somewhere in the basement.

He sighed and eased his big body into the chair. Blinking from sleepiness he rolled a last cigarette before going to bed, and looked at his watch. It was long after midnight. He yawned noisily, stretched, and unfastened his collar and tie.

What a day. One investigation after another. A grilling, a murder, charges and counter-charges. And then, as if that wasn't enough, an attempted frame.

A lousy profession. He ought to be a banker or a preacher. Then life would flow smoothly. There wouldn't be all these treacherous eddies to struggle against. At least his life would have the semblance of honesty. As it was he was always looked upon with suspicion by the police, and quite frankly detested by the District Attorney and his staff of investigators.

Grand Juries regarded him as an actual menace. His enemies with white hatred. His friends, those he knew would be loyal in any emergency, might be counted on the fingers of one hand—Etta, Matt Ridley, Esther, the girl at the switchboard downstairs. And he'd have one finger left over.

The cigarette smoke felt good going into his lungs.

It helped him to relax. Line by line the tenseness went out of his round face as he slumped deeper into the chair. All kinds of thoughts began to march like small figurines across the back of his eyes.

He thought of the man Leahy, and wondered how far he could trust him. Not too far, just yet. But far enough for all practical purposes. Yes, Leahy was all right.

His head sagged back against the softness of the chair. Eyes drooped shut. Funny about that insurance policy. No beneficiary named except in the clause of a will. Was it possible that Gillespie, granting that he wasn't dead, had evolved a scheme of collecting the premium himself?

If so, figuring the amount of the premium, the cash received for the house in Los Gatos canyon, and the two hundred thousand of outright theft from Anderson's account, somebody, if not Gillespie was making a haul of close to a quarter of a million dollars. And anyone getting in the path of the murderers was simply flirting with death.

And what of that smooth attorney, George Baron? Where did he come into the picture of embezzlement and crime? By tomorrow he hoped to have the answer. Matt would phone from Ohio. Esther would have her London report. And Leahy, granting he was lucky and clever enough, might obtain . . .

At this point his thoughts left him, and the figurines marching across the back of his eyes disappeared into the limbo of forgotten things on business of their own. His cigarette dropped in a dull shower of sparks from thumb and forefinger, bounced off the chair cushion, smouldered to the carpet and went out.

Somewhere in a neighboring apartment, a clock chimed a single sweet note—one-thirty. The coastal city was once more preparing for bed.

Outside there was a full moon overhead, but a wet ground fog had rolled in from the Pacific and dimmed its brilliance. Distant buildings weaved in the fog like pale, half-formed cenotaphs out of some forgotten graveyard.

Only a thin luminescence pierced the fog. The iron slats on the fire-escape dripped moisture. And the slats stood out in serried ranks of gleaming metal beneath the back window of Crole's apartment.

Two men stood on the metal cross-pieces. One of them was doing something with the window catch. The sharp snap of the fastener breaking was gobbled up by the night.

The window slid upward. The two men straddled the sill. There was a faint rustle of cloth, and they were inside the apartment. They did not close the window.

Simon Crole roused up. He blinked once. Then all sleep left him, for he was staring into the muzzles of two guns held rigidly on his unmoving body.

"Who the hell let you in?" he said, crossly.

Gene Selingo grinned. "Tell him, Ghost."

Ghost Mokund grunted a single syllable. "Ummm!"

CHAPTER XIII

CROLE TAKES A RIDE

GENE SELINGO continued to grin, and the grin was like a wide gash extending from ear to ear. "We got in," he said, "the same way as we're going out."

"You can go any time now," said Crole. "I don't need you."

"But we need you. See? You're altogether too smart a dick for this town. You're beginning to get in people's way. But maybe you've figured this already."

"Sore because I busted in the hotel room late this afternoon?"

"My jaw and face still ache from those wallops you handed me. Why shouldn't I be sore? Damn right I am. And when I get sore I get mean all over."

"I'm that way, too," observed Crole.

"The hell with you. Get up out of that chair. You're going with us—for a nice long ride."

"I don't want to ride. I want to go to sleep."

"You'll sleep, brother. And it'll be the longest sleep you ever had. In fact there won't be no end to it."

An atavistic craving to knock the heads of these unwelcome visitors together sent Crole lunging to his feet. Gene Selingo moved in close, snarling and eager. His gun was level with the agency man's chest.

Ghost Mokund glided sinuously in a half circle until he was behind Crole. They had him covered from two angles. He couldn't move forward or back without running into a leaden slug.

"Get the notion out of your head, Crole, that there's any way you can get out of it. You can't—except by a stretcher. Coming with us or do we have to mess up the place?"

Simon Crole was placid once more. The hot uprush of anger at seeing these men left him as rapidly as it had come. In its place returned cunning and guile.

"What have you boys got against me?" he wanted to know.

"Never mind," snapped Selingo, "what we got against you. It ain't necessary to explain. You're simply coming with us. See? And you're coming carefully and without any false starts. We're leaving the way we came—by the fire-escape. Ghost, you go first. Crole, you stay in the middle and I'll be close behind you. Got it straight?"

Crole nodded.

"Then start moving."

"I think," said Crole, "that there's a half pint of Scotch in the radio bar. Mind taking it along with us? A guy should be entitled to at least one drink on this long ride you're telling about."

Selingo backed to the radio cabinet and found the half pint of Scotch. "Not a bad idea at all," he beamed, tucking it in his pocket.

"I feel better already," observed Crole, following Mokund through the kitchen window onto the fire-escape.

If he had expected to make a break while going down the metal structure, he was doomed to disappointment. Never once were their guns pointed on any spot but his body. In single file they moved through the fog in the alley back of the apartment house. At the first corner they turned right and stopped beside a low-slung car.

The light, in spite of the fog wavering around street lamps, was sufficient to enable Crole to observe the tires. They were new Generals, the same kind of tires as were on the car that had forced Gillespie's machine from the Iron Mountain road.

Mokund got in first. Laid his gun handy beside him on the seat and got in behind the wheel. Crole climbed into the rear seat, the barrel of Selingo's gun prodding him cruelly.

Sighing, he relaxed and faced the man beside him. "Where you taking me?"

Selingo sat with one leg doubled under him so that he faced the agency man. His right wrist rested on the knee of the leg that was curled beneath him. The barrel pointed straight at Crole's side. He made no answer.

"Getting tongue-tied, like the punk on the front seat?"

Mokund, dexterously heading the car out towards a main trunk boulevard, made no comment. Selingo snapped: "We're taking you to the desert, fellow. And when we get there we're going to dump you out."

"Nice boat," approved Crole. "What'll she do on the level?"

"Plenty."

"Mind if I reach in my pocket for the makings? I'm dying for a smoke."

Selingo fished a cigarette from his pocket, lighted it and passed it to the detective. "You'll just about have time to smoke it," he said quietly.

Crole puffed contentedly, and watched the road on the right side. His apartment house was well on the outer fringe of the city and the low-slung car was making good speed.

The car eased into a four-lane boulevard and started up a slight grade. Its powerful headlights cut a wide arc in the roadway. Crole, his eyes noting each familiar landmark, said: "What'll I do with the butt?"

"Step on it, and don't try to pull anything."

The detective dropped the butt to the floor and placed his heel on it. "You two guys are strangers in this town."

"Does it matter?"

"I never saw you before today."

"We move around some," said Selingo.

"Making lots of jack?"

"None of your damn business. We ain't talking."

"Pass through Needles coming into the state?"

"Listen, Crole. Sure we come through Needles. But it's no good. Thinking about the cops at the border, hey? Well, they let us through. Why shouldn't they? We had plenty. It's only the poor bums that get turned back."

The car reached an intersection, hesitated only a bare fraction of a second, then slid across. Beyond the intersection about a mile, a narrow county road ran off to the right. The car swerved onto the narrow road.

"Made a wrong turn, you at the wheel," said Crole. "The desert road goes straight ahead."

"Ummm!" grunted Mokund.

"He says to mind your own business," Selingo interpreted.

"This road we're on now," continued Crole, "used to be the old road before they cut through the new one. And it goes up through Los Gatos canyon."

"It's our road," said Selingo, "And there's no use trying to figure it."

"If you're about ready to fill my frame with lead, it'd make it a lot easier if I had an edge on. Maybe you hoods know how it feels to be in a spot like I am. Maybe you don't. But take my word for it—it's hell. How's for a shot of Scotch?"

Selingo's free hand fished the bottle from his coat pocket. "Slow down, Ghost," he ordered. "This is as good a spot as any. No traffic. And no houses."

The car slackened its speed to about twenty miles an hour as it crawled up the grade and ran along a fairly level ridge.

"Drink, Crole. And when the liquor is gone, unless it takes more than three minutes, you'll go with it."

Simon Crole's hand shook as he reached for the bottle. "I'm not feeling so hot. I'll do the best I can. Three minutes is too short a time to properly enjoy a drink. And I don't like to swill."

"Quit monkeying around!" This was Mokund making a long speech from the front seat.

"Geez!" gasped the agency man. "How that guy scared me! I didn't think he could talk." He held the neck of the bottle to his lips and drank long and deeply. Coming up for air he swayed and looked slightly stupid.

"Sorry," he apologized.

Selingo began to cautiously shift his position as he reached for a second cigarette. Again lifting the bottle to his lips, the agency man made a pretense of swallowing. But all he did was to fill his mouth to capacity with the fiery liquor.

Although facing straight ahead, his eyes were swiveled far to his left where dimly, in the soft glow of the instrument panel light, he could see Selingo making ready to snap the wheel of his lighter.

The lighter broke into sudden flame. There came a moment of total blindness as the lighter traveled towards the cigarette. Timed to the split second, the whiskey left Crole's mouth in a wooshing spray. It struck Selingo full in the face, burned into his eyes and drenched the lighter flame.

With the same movement Crole flung his body in a half-roll. There was thunder in his ears—three sharp peals, mingling with long spurts of flame. The first bullet took a hot chunk out of his arm. The second tore through the sleeve farther up. The third missed completely and made a neat hole through the shatter-proof glass of the rear-vision window.

And Simon Crole, his back to the front seat, reached out and grabbed at a point in back of those streaking flames. His fingers closed over Selingo's forearm, slid to the wrist, then tightened down and twisted sharply.

Selingo's big mouth dribbled curses. He kicked Crole in the shins, then in the chest and face. Stung with pain, the agency man got his feet beneath him and raised up.

He smacked Selingo in the mouth and cut his knuckles badly. But he still hung fast to the wrist above the gunman's fingers. Mokund, steering with one hand, twisted around, grabbed up his gun by its squat barrel and swung with the butt at Crole's head.

Crole raised his shoulder, took the blow on bunched muscles, and butted his head against Selingo's neck. The gunman went limp and began to cough. The detective jerked the weapon from unresisting fingers.

Mokund, meanwhile, had reversed his grip on the automatic, and his finger was squeezing on the trigger. Crole flattened, and the leaden pellets passed over his head. He pawed for the door handle, found it and exerted a downward pressure. The weight of his body sent the door swinging outward. He got one foot ahead of him. It hit the running board. Lead was singing past his ears, powder burning the back of his neck.

His right foot left the running board just as his left foot struck the shoulder of the road. And the car was moving just fast enough to throw him off balance.

For a moment of eternity he hung poised, spun from momentum, and went plunging down into the black abyss that was Los Gatos canyon.

Ghost Mokund jerked on the emergency brake and leaped to the canyon rim. He pointed his gun in the direction of the falling body and emptied the shell clip of his gun.

The thrashings of the rolling body came up to him, growing fainter and fainter. And then there was no sound to be heard but the soft purr of the car motor and the retching of Gene Selingo as he became violently ill kneeling in the center of the lonely road.

Ghost Mokund ejected a short, ugly word and bent over his companion in crime. "Sick?"

Selingo gagged and made horrible noises. He was sick all right. But not fatally. He'd be all right in ten minutes. He was too tough to be sick longer than that.

Mokund walked to the edge of the road and again stared down into blackness. Far in the distance he heard the strident voice of a hungry coyote wailing its misery. He shuddered. Reached into his pocket for a thin paper packet.

He poured the white powder from the packet onto the back of his hand and sniffed it with something like a sob in his breath. At peace once more, he went back to Selingo who was crawling back towards the car.

"Tough guy," he said.

Selingo groaned with misery. "Whiskey. See if there's any left in the bottle."

Mokund poked around, found it and pressed the bottle's neck to his companion's slobbering mouth. After a few moments the sick man, still breathing raspingly said: "Which way did he go?"

Mokund pointed down into the velvety black of the steep canyon wall. He also showed with a slight shrug the empty clip from his automatic.

"We'll come out," gasped Selingo, "early in the morning and make sure. Geez, how my neck aches. Turn around and let's go back to town. I ain't equal to facing the big guy tonight."

Mokund evidently was of the same opinion. Deftly he cramped the car around on the narrow road, and headed it downgrade towards the distant lights of the coastal city.

A new day was graying the sky in the east when Simon Crole plodded through the front door of his apartment house. His face was dust-covered and bloody. His eyes, heavy-lidded and slightly bulgy. The backs of his hands were lacerated from contact with mahogany and manzanita bushes that had checked his sudden descent into the canyon and saved his life. His suit was fit only for carpet rags.

He tried to smile at the switchboard girl who was staring at him with pained eyes of compassion. "Oh my God, Mr. Crole. You're hurt. Something awful's happened . . ."

The big body of the agency man swayed. He reached out a hand and steadied himself against the switchboard. But the smile wouldn't come. He brushed a hand wearily across his eyes. Every bone in his body pulsed with an intolerable ache.

"Any calls for me while I've been gone?" he husked.

"You poor, stupid man," wailed the girl. "This is no time to make wise cracks. Get right up to your apartment. I'll call a doctor. I'll . . ."

"No, dear," said Crole. "I'm okay. I look worse than I feel. Couple of punks took me for a scenic ride. I got tired of the scenery, hauled out my roller skates and came back home—only I fell down a mountain on account I wasn't used to the skates."

The girl did something to the switchboard. "I'll help you to your door," she said. "But I wish you'd let me call a doctor."

"Nix on the doctor stuff. Just give me an arm up the stairs, sister, and I'll be your pal for life."

The steps conquered, he fumbled for his key. "What time is it?"

"Five-thirty."

"Swell. I'll have time for a couple hours' sleep. You go off duty when?"

"At seven. But I'll leave word with the day operator to call you at . . ."

"Half past eight."

The door pushed inward. "You going to be all right?" she asked.

"A hot bath, a change of clothes and I'll be the adonis of crime and the envy of the police department. Scram, little one, and keep your lips buttoned up."

He closed the door and went straight to the radio cabinet. His lips puckered at its emptiness. Nothing but gin. He disliked it. But he drank some—half a tumbler.

Warmed, he stripped and went into the bathroom. The needle shower of scalding water stung his body into a glow. He used soap liberally, rinsed and finished with cold water.

Standing before a mirror after he had rubbed himself dry, he surveyed the welts and bruises on his body. There was a chunk of flesh gone from his arm. He swabbed it with iodine and covered it with adhesive tape.

Then, clad in a lounging robe, he went into the kitchen, scowled at the broken catch on the rear window and brewed himself some strong coffee. He drank the coffee, smoked a cigarette, and afterwards stretched out on the bed. Sleep came instantly, like a warm comforting anaesthesia.

George Baron removed a ten-dollar note from his billfold, smiled at the Commodore porter, and said: "And you say his trunks are to be delivered to the Hotel Franklin, on San Felice street?"

"Yes, sir," replied the porter, keeping his eye on the money.

"That's fine." He extended the bill.

The porter took it. "Thank you, sir."

"Quite all right," nodded George Baron, turning away.

He arrived at the Franklin at half past eight. Talked with the operator at the switchboard, and was again liberal with his largess.

Anderson came down after a few minutes, pale and disheveled. He looked with suspicious eyes at the well-dressed attorney. "I thought it was Simon down here," he said.

"No," smiled Baron. "Simon couldn't come. So he sent me. I work for him."

"I've never seen you around."

"True, but the fact remains I'm in Crole's employ. Otherwise I wouldn't have come to this hotel. He was the only one in the city who knew where you were registered."

"That's right," nodded Anderson. "Well, what is it you want?"

"I'm taking you to a place in Los Gatos canyon."

"Oh! What's the idea?"

"Simon Crole is there. With him is a young lady—Virginia Laird."

"Why didn't you say so in the first place? Then she *was* kidnapped after all. And that wire from Kansas City was . . ."

"Crole's orders were not to explain things, but to bring you to a certain house you're undoubtedly familiar with."

"Well," snapped Anderson, suddenly impatient to see the girl again, "what are we waiting for?"

While this interesting event was taking place, Simon Crole was being awakened by the insistent ringing of his telephone. He groaned in the spirit as he thought of the day's tasks—tasks he knew would further drain his vitality.

He dressed with care, called a taxi and was driven downtown. Wary from past experiences, he ate his breakfast before doing anything else. Then, stepping jauntily, he entered his office.

"Morning, precious," he greeted his secretary, sweeping his hat from his bald head in an exaggerated gesture. "I see you've opened the place on time. Any callers?"

Etta looked up from a ledger. "You been in a train wreck?"

"No train wreck. I got tangled up in the city flesh-pots and a couple of them got busted."

"You have all the marks of a hangover. Captain Jorgens phoned twice this morning. He seems a little concerned." She handed him a yellow envelope. "Telegram from Matt. I read it, but didn't call you about it since I knew you would be down in time. You'll also find José Hernandez inside. He's been here since eight this morning. Anything special you want me to do?"

"Yeah. Call the manager of my apartment house. Tell him that there's a busted catch on the back kitchen window. Also call Captain Jorgens. Tell him I'll be down to see him—after a while."

He hung up his hat and moved into his private office rubbing his palms together. "Mr. Hernandez," he said. "The old Don himself. I'm glad to see you. I was coming out to your place sometime this morning."

"Ha, Señor Crole. I am pleased. My boy Manuel is a changed man. He is indeed. He has gone to work harvesting walnuts. He will be a success. Of that I am assured. I wish to give you money. Never can it be said that José Hernandez is ungrateful."

"Sit down, José. I don't want your money. Put it back in your pant's pocket. In fact I want you to take *my* money."

José Hernandez went on the defensive. His jet eyes became sly. He rubbed the rough texture of his chocolate brown suit. "You give José Hernandez money? I am a man of business, Señor Crole. A Mexican, yes. But I have the education. When the Americano says he will give me money, I take pause. I am alert like the coyote. I wait for further explanations."

"In my business I encounter strange situations," explained Crole. "There is, José, in Los Gatos Canyon, an estate with a house on it. A large house with many rooms. It was formerly owned by a gentleman named Anderson. The house was sold."

"So long as you do not wish to sell it to me," began José . . .

"Attend carefully, José, while I explain. This house, so I am told, is empty except for a caretaker and his family. The caretaker, I am also informed, is a Mexican like yourself."

"Ha!" breathed Hernandez.

"Should," continued Crole, "a gentleman of your ability appear at this estate, guarded by one of your own country-men, I have reason to believe that you could learn whether this big house is empty or not. And if anyone is living in it—who they might be. Is the task too great?"

"There would be the expense of hiring a man to watch my business for the day," said José Hernandez, "and the expense of a second man to watch the first. Seven dollars should be the expense. Four for the first man. Three for the second. I should also be cheated in spite of this arrangement to the ex-tent of three more dollars."

"That," said Crole, "is a matter entirely yours. If you'll go to this house, acquaint yourself with the caretaker, and find out what I wish to know, I will free you of the ten dollars you already owe me, and give you twenty-five dollars addi-tional. I will also arrange the transportation and pay for it so that it will not cost you a penny."

"*Esta bien!*" agreed Hernandez, nodding vigorously. "But there is the matter of a friendship token."

"The bribe. Of course. Will ten bucks cover it?"

"Of course, sure!"

"Okay. You go home and change your clothes. That's a pretty loud outfit you're wearing. Put on some old clothes. And I'll send a cab to your place. The driver will know where to take you. And you can arrange with him when to pick you up. Now beat it home, José. The cab will pick you up in half an hour. You got it clear in your head what I want you to do?"

"The big house," said José, checking off the points on his fingers, "is empty." He checked off the second point. "The big house is also not empty. There is someone inside. It is your wish to know who is there, and how many there are of him."

"That's correct."

José got to his feet. "*Adios.* I will return with a report with a quick promptness."

As the man in the chocolate brown suit vanished into the hall, Crole read Matt Ridley's telegram.

REPORT NEARLY COMPLETE STOP WILL PHONE YOU TEN O'CLOCK PACIFIC STANDARD TIME STOP BE THERE RIDLEY

Crole laid the telegram down and looked at his watch. It was ten minutes to ten. He took down the receiver and called a number. To the voice answering he said: "Send Scavillo to my office, will you. Tell him to leave his cab outside and come up. I'm in a hurry. Right. G'bye."

He hung up and went into his front office. "Precious," he said. "Hernandez is working for me. Also there is an agency man, former partner of Coughlin, named Leahy, down on our payroll. So be nice to these new boys . . ."

The telephone rang sharply. Etta lifted the receiver. A voice said: "Lima operator calling Spring Six—thrrree—"

"It's Matt!" whispered Etta. "Take it in your own office."

Crole went hurriedly to his desk. Sat down, and lifted the receiver from the hook. There was some small confusion on the line, and out of it came Matt Ridley's clear voice. "Hello, boss! Matt! You hear me?"

"Yeah," said Crole. "Go slow for a few seconds." He raised his eyes. In the doorway stood bleak-faced Captain Jorgens, scowling as usual, and plucking at his black mustache.

"Have a chair, Captain," invited the agency man. "It's the Captain, Matt. He just came in. Go ahead. What was it you were saying?"

"Don't let me bother you," came gruffly from the police officer. "I've got all day to hang around. So has the Commis-

sioner and the Mayor. We're only poorly paid public officials . . ."

"Save it," said Crole. "I can't listen to two people at the
same time, and this call is costing me money."

Jorgens shut up, took a cigar from his pocket, regarded it
tentatively, then thrust it back in his pocket. He started to sit
down on the leather couch, saw the dark stains, and wandered over towards a chair near the window. Easing himself
into it he began to crack his knuckles.

CHAPTER XIV

MURDER BY SUBSTITUTION

SIMON CROLE, HIS FACE IMPASSIVE as he listened to his operator's report over the long-distance wire, said: "Is that all, Matt?"

"All?" crackled Ridley's voice. "What more do you want? Maybe you think I haven't been sweating since I went to work. My legs have shrunk half an inch from walking from one place to another."

"You did excellent, Matt. I'll carry on now from this end. Take the next train . . ."

"Me, ride on a lousy train? I already got my seat paid for on a fast air liner. I'll be home in one short time. Bye."

"Bye." Crole hung up. Jorgens stirred in his chair and began to clear his throat.

The phone tinkled. Crole took down the receiver and heard Etta's honeyed voice say: "Scavillo is out in the hall."

"Excuse me, Captain," said the agency man. "This seems to be my busy day. Be back in half a minute." It was nearly five minutes before he got back. During the absence Jorgens' temper hadn't improved. "You're like a flea, Simon, the way you keep jumping around. Light somewhere, damn you, so I can get a few things off my mind."

"You cops," said Crole, grunting as he slumped into his comfortable chair, "are all alike. Always cranky, always in a hurry. I've got some ancient Bourbon, Captain. I'll not offer you any because I don't think you'd care for it."

Jorgens said testily: "Hell with your Bourbon. I've got other things to do."

"You haven't, by any chance," broke in Crole, "found the solution to the so-called Gillespie murder, have you?"

"Nor the Coughlin shooting, either. But I have a fair idea that the solution is nearer than you think. And I'm beginning to see eye to eye with the District Attorney . . ."

"You two men will never see eye to eye in anything. And you know it. It's always been my contention, Captain, that the police should do the outside work in a murder case, and that the D.A. should do the prosecuting."

"I believe I've heard you say some such thing."

"If we're still friends, you'll share some Bourbon with me. Otherwise I'll drink alone and think alone. And when I have the solutions of these two murders on a platter, I'll pass the platter to the man above you."

Jorgens lunged to his feet and came over to the desk. "Give me that Bourbon," he said. "I'll drink it, Simon, not because I regard you as a friend, but because I like it as well as you do."

Crole sighed. "It's a roundabout way of saying we're still friends, but I guess it's as much as I can hope for from an eternally suspicious police officer like you."

"All right, all right. But what about these solutions on a platter. Who killed Gillespie? Who . . .?"

"One at a time, Captain. Everybody, including yourself, seems to be laboring under an erroneous impression. James Gillespie, I have every reason to believe, is not dead."

Jorgens appeared to choke. His face became beet red. His eyes watered. Otherwise he was quite calm. "The papers said he was murdered. The medical examiner . . ."

"We won't get anywhere, Captain, if you're going to start contradicting everything I say. Now listen and don't get yourself in a dither. I haven't any real proof, but I expect to have it by tonight."

"I knew there was a catch in it somewhere," complained Jorgens.

"There is a man in this case," continued Crole, evenly, "who has not yet appeared in the investigations. His name is Edward Smith of Lima, Ohio. He was of the same general size and weight of Gillespie, and looked like him. He was a law clerk, an excellent poker player, and without work until he received a letter directing him to come at once to this city where a position awaited him. He . . ."

"Wait a second, Simon. Where did you learn . . .?"

"Matt Ridley's been in Smith's home town doing a little private investigating. Maybe you heard him telling me most of this over the phone a few minutes ago."

"I heard nothing except your big mouth saying 'yeah' and 'ahuh'."

"Smith's brother got a card mailed at Williams, Arizona, saying that he, Edward Smith, had lost his car. Somebody had stolen it. That was the last word the brother heard from Edward Smith."

"Hmmmm! I'm a long ways from understanding the connection between Smith and Gillespie."

"All right. We'll get closer to home. Coughlin, as a private detective, was hired by Gillespie and others. Coughlin got to know too much. So he was destroyed. Dying in this office, he tried to tell me who killed him and failed. But he did say something about Edward Smith being Gillespie's double. That's why I went to the expense of sending Ridley east by plane to check from the other end. And our next checking point will have to be on the border at Needles. That's where you come in."

"You mean," said Jorgens, beginning to see a little light, "that Smith reached California on foot, and came to this city?"

"Exactly."

"Ummm. How long ago do you figure that Smith crossed the border into California?"

"Three days ago, maybe four. The card he wrote to his brother was post-marked the 11th. The man who was supposed to be Gillespie was killed on the 15th." Jorgens examined his knuckles. "The dates are all right. But the actual facts are a long ways from . . ."

"Didn't your men at the border check on everybody coming in? If they did, there should be some sort of record on Edward Smith. He had a letter with him. That letter promised him a job. He wouldn't get turned back at the border."

"I get the point," said Jorgens. "Let me see. I shifted the men on duty at the border only yesterday. None of them liked the work. I couldn't blame them. And those who were on duty when Smith came through are here in the city. Sergeant Breen was in charge. He ought to know."

He sat down on the desk, picked up Crole's phone and called Headquarters. "Lieutenant," he said to the man who answered. "Get in touch with Sergeant Breen and send him at once to the office of Simon Crole. I'll be here, waiting. Move fast. It's serious."

He turned on Crole again. "What else you got on your mind?"

Crole blinked sleepily. "I almost forgot, Captain. The murder car that forced Gillespie's machine from the road was an Auburn sedan, leather-covered seats, dark red, a late model and General tires on all four wheels."

"That's more like it."

"The driver," Crole went on, "has a wan face, boyish, and has all the characteristics of a dope addict. His nickname is Ghost. The second of this pair is about my build, thick lips, a wide mouth, and is very, very tough. I have an idea that they once belonged to some eastern mob that's been scattered by state and federal men. I don't know, of course. But they don't belong on this coast. They were imported by . . ."

"Yeah. Who?"

Simon Crole smiled evasively. "I was going to say somebody. Actually I don't know. That's another task for your office to uncover."

"Who sent Edward Smith the letter bringing him here?"

"I wouldn't know that, Captain. Ridley couldn't find out."

"I'll get a report out on the teletype describing the car and the two men driving it. Unless it's in a garage we ought to have it by tonight."

Once more he talked into the phone describing the murder car and its occupants. When he had finished he said: "That report will flash in all station houses, and go over the air to all our squad cars. Now that we know what to look for, we'll find it—and damned quick."

"There's a Sergeant Breen here," called Etta from the front office.

"Come in, Sergeant," growled Jorgens. "You acquainted with this private dick? Well, it's time you were. He's the head of this agency. A sly, tricky man who knows his way around. But don't ever fully trust him or he'll cheat you out of your life savings. Simon, meet Sergeant Breen."

The two men shook hands, measured each other and grinned.

"Have a chair, Sergeant," invited Crole.

Breen sat down, his eyes slightly puzzled.

"Listen," began Captain Jorgens. "We're checking on a man named Edward Smith who came west from Lima, Ohio. Sometime between the 11th and 14th he must have passed through your barrier. Remember him?"

"Remember a Smith?" asked Breen. "Hundreds of Smiths went through while I was on duty. I couldn't remember . . ."

"To be specific," Crole cut in. "This man Smith probably came through alone. He was a law clerk, and he lost his car at Williams, Arizona. He carried with him a letter from . . ."

"Oh, sure!" nodded Breen. "I know the man you mean. He came up to the barrier on foot right after I checked through an Auburn with New York license plates . . ."

"Hold everything," said Jorgens, leaning forward. "An Auburn, did you say? And did you notice its tires?"

"Are we talking about Smith or is it something else? I started to tell you . . ."

"Yes, Sergeant, you're doing fine. I still want to hear about this Smith, but when you mentioned that Auburn, you unintentionally gave us an unusual tip. Do you remember who was in the car?"

"Couple of hard-looking men I thought at the time. But they had plenty of money. In fact they passed me a twenty and I turned it over to the chow fund at the Desert Inn to help feed the poor bums we had to turn back."

Jorgens rubbed his palms briskly. "I'm banking on that memory of yours, Sergeant. Now we'll get back to Smith. He

had a letter promising him a job in the coastal city. You recall the letter?"

"Damn right. He wanted to read it to me, but I said I could
read plenty good. It said his qualifications were good and he
was expected not later than the 15th."

Captain Jorgens shot a quick glance at the agency man. But
Simon Crole was staring impassively at the lithograph of the
Darktown Fire Brigade.

"Who signed the letter?" barked Jorgens.

Sergeant Breen pursed his lips, frowned, and his eyes went
vacant. "I don't remember," he said, uneasily.

Jorgens pounded the desk with a clenched hand. "Damn it,
Sergeant, you've got to remember. Concentrate! The signature is important. It holds the clue to a couple of murders."

"I'm trying to think," said Breen. "I can see the letter plain.
And the date, and that part about the qualifications. Ain't it
the berries how the name eludes me."

Jorgens got to his feet, his face working. "That!" he raged,
pointing to the sergeant and fixing Crole with a bleak stare,
"is what I have working for me. He sees a name. And he
can't remember. He's paid to remember such things. He's
even trained. He's an ordinary cop when I recommend him
for a sergeancy. And this is what he tells me: 'Ain't it the
berries how the name eludes me.' Nothing's ever going to be
right from now on. I can feel it in my bones."

"Finished?" asked Crole, stifling a yawn.

"All right," snapped Jorgens. "You go on from where I left
off. Ask the sergeant . . ."

"Take it easy, Captain. Breen knows the name. Just because he can't say it when you start screaming at him is no
sign he won't remember it. Sit down, will you. You're wearing out my floor."

He swung on Breen and smiled warmly. "Sergeant, I want
you to forget what you saw on that letter. We'll get at it by
another method—the method of association.

"Now listen. I suggest this desk. What do you immediately
think of? Answer quick."

"Blotter, typewriter . . ."

"Good. Try this one: Siren."

"Police."

"Murder."

"Coughlin case . . ." He hesitated, looked foolish and said without conscious thought: "Gillespie."

"Ummm!" grunted Crole.

"So help me!" said Breen, somewhat startled. "That's the name, Gillespie! I remember it now. The name is James Gillespie."

"Observe," said Crole, "how beautifully the idea of association works in the mind of an intelligent officer."

"If the sergeant wasn't a trusted and capable law-enforcer, Simon, I'd say you were kidding me."

"You would. But Sergeant Breen does not work for me. He's your man—not mine."

"All right," conceded Jorgens. "But we're still right where we were a few minutes ago. What's the reason back of all this?"

"The *modus operandi*," said Crole, "is simple—greed for another man's wealth—a sum in excess of two hundred thousand dollars. The plan was simplicity itself. When James Gillespie saw the possibilities of becoming the owner of this small fortune, he cast about for a safe method. To abscond openly was not to be considered.

"What does he do? He finds a man in the middle west who closely resembles him. Brings him to this city with an offer of a job. Arranges with this man to drive his car to a certain place. Gives him his keys and other things. Then hires two men to destroy him so that the killing would appear accidental.

"Edward Smith of Lima, Ohio was selected for this purpose. And Edward Smith now lies in the morgue under the name of James Gillespie, a victim of a rather gruesome murder—murder by substitution. Which leaves Gillespie in the clear."

"Are you talking about the Gillespie who was murdered?" asked Sergeant Breen, innocently.

"My God," complained Crole. "Have I got to go through all this again? Yes, it's the same man. The smart boys on the press made a little mistake aided and abetted by the police."

"At your suggestion," said Jorgens, drily.

"What I said," argued Crole, "was that the victim found in the car was murdered. I never mentioned Gillespie."

"Enough!" snapped Jorgens. "I'll uncover Gillespie if he's still in the city. I'll also get a description of Smith, finger prints if he has any and birth marks. And I'll know damn soon who this cadaver is we're still holding at the morgue."

"Who is this fellow Smith you keep talking about?" asked Breen. "Is he the same Smith who came through the barrier? 'cause if he is I'll know him."

"Even if his face and torso are badly burned?" quizzed Jorgens.

"I've got something better than that. The little finger on his right hand was cut off at the first joint."

Captain Jorgens actually beamed. "Sergeant, I was all ready to call you a poor, dumb flatfoot. I'm glad I didn't." He picked up the phone once more and called his office, issued a brief order and seated himself on the desk while he waited. When the captain set the phone down again his face was once more wearing its funeral wreath of official dignity.

"The corpse at the morgue," he said, "is undoubtedly that of Edward Smith. Breen's sharp eyes have established an identification that will have to be further verified. But it looks like we're on the right track."

"That's fine," approved Crole. "It seems that we have reached an amicable understanding with each other for once."

"You may understand me, Simon. But I'll be damned if I understand you or your methods. Listen. I called the Commodore. It was necessary that I get Ned Anderson down to headquarters to explain his relations . . ."

Crole broke in, shaking his head slowly back and forth: "You see, Captain, my client left the Commodore yesterday. In fact I, personally, moved him out because his life was threatened."

Jorgens' eyes became speculative. "So? You never told me a word about this."

"Of course I didn't. It didn't seem necessary. I took Anderson to another hotel farther from the center of town. Those two hoods were . . . well, I got there just in time to save him from drinking whiskey doped with Cyanid of potassium they were going to make him swallow. I came out second best in the fight that followed, but he didn't drink any of the poison."

"You must be slipping, Simon."

"I guess I am. Now I'll present a few more points of interest."

Jorgens nodded. "I think you'd better present them all, Simon."

"At the right time, Captain. You know me, or you should by this time. Have you ever been left out of an arrest on any of my cases?"

"Never."

"All right. Just to keep the record straight, Miss Laird had reasons to believe Gillespie, with his power of attorney, was slowly draining Anderson's bank account of its available cash. When Anderson arrived at our coastal city she, on her own responsibility, went to him and acquainted him with the facts. Someone suspected her and had her followed. The man who shadowed her was Coughlin. He evidently had orders to get her away from Anderson. A snatch was attempted. Anderson butted in and broke it up.

"You've already read the portion of a note the girl wrote him. And you've probably accepted the fact that the girl is in the east. I'd like to believe it, Captain. But I can't. The telegram received by the girl's mother seemed genuine, and was. But its contents might have been faked. Gillespie, and others, are nothing if not determined to protect themselves. And they'll not stop at one murder—or two. I think Anderson will be safe if he stays inside the hotel. He promised me he would. Nothing but a direct order from me will take him out to the street."

"If you think he's positively in danger," said Jorgens, "I can send a couple of my men to his hotel. Between them they can watch the hall and his door."

"Maybe you'd better," sighed Crole. "He's a trusting sort of individual, and I'm not under-rating the brains of Gillespie and those men working with him. But wait, I'll call him and tell him about the officers you plan to send to the hotel."

He thumbed the telephone directory, found the Franklin on San Felice and spoke the number. "Mr. Anderson's room, please."

"Sorry," answered the hotel operator. "Mr. Anderson left early this morning. A gentleman, a friend of his called. They left together. Is there any message you'd like to leave, sir?"

"None," said Crole, shaking his head dejectedly. He hung up.

Captain Jorgens sniffed. "Well? Are we too late?" Crole nodded. "Yeah. Too late. And to think that Anderson promised me he wouldn't stir from the hotel unless I ordered . . ." He checked suddenly and his mouth began to twitch. Abruptly he called the hotel again and said to the switchboard operator: "I just finished talking with you about one of your guests, a Mr. Anderson. Remember?"

"Yes. What is it, please?"

"You told me he left with a friend. Could you describe the man?"

"Who is this calling?"

"Police Department," said Crole, throwing a quick glance at Captain Jorgens.

"He seemed like a middle-aged man," said the operator. "Well-dressed, gray mustache. I don't remember anything else about him."

"I see. But did he give any name when he asked you to phone Mr. Anderson?"

"Oh yes. We always take names in cases where we make calls." There followed a slight pause as the operator consulted her list of calls made. "Waiting?"

"Yes," said the agency man.

"The man who went away with Mr. Anderson gave the name of Simon Crole. That's all I know, sir."

"Thanks. It's enough." Again he hung up. "The description she gave of the man whom Anderson left with," lied Crole, for reasons of his own, "is of no help. But the name he gave is quite familiar. It was Simon Crole."

Captain Jorgens searched for a cigar to chew on. Found one, and clamped it between his teeth. "Simon Crole, eh. Been walking in your sleep?"

"Hardly."

Captain Jorgens frowned heavily. "Sergeant Breen," he stated, "you're to forget everything you have overheard in this office until the proper time comes. Simon, this case is getting top-heavy. Two murders, now a kidnapping. You've got to draw in the strings. I've gone with you as far as I dare without getting myself in trouble with the District Attorney's office."

"I know all that, Captain. And it's got me slightly worried."

"Slightly? You'd better take this thing serious. The D.A. is in a black mood. In case you don't know it, there is a reform movement yammering for a clean-up in city politics— especially the police and public prosecutor's offices."

"I'm not concerned with the District Attorney," said Crole. "He's out to get my license revoked. Maybe he'll succeed. He's an honest and sincere public official. And so are you, Captain. Neither of you could be bribed. But the D.A. thinks I'm crooked. And he won't rest easy till he closes my office."

"You've got him all wrong, Simon."

"Okay. I've got a lot of things to do, Captain. And so have you. Let's quit this harangue before we both lose our tempers."

"I'll be in my office all day, Simon—close to the phone."

"That's fine. Keep your big car ready. I may need help before the next twelve hours."

"You mean . . ."

"I mean the showdown's close. I've been pushed around all I intend to be. Now I'm going to start pushing myself. G'bye. And remember what I said about keeping your big car ready."

Jorgens nodded, looked as if he might say something more, then signaled Breen. Together they left the office.

"It's about time," scolded Etta.

Crole looked up inquiringly. "You telling *me?*"

"Yes, boss, I'm telling *you.* Esther has been in the woman's room out in the hall for the past half hour waiting for you to get through with your heart-to-heart talk with the police."

"Shocking!" grinned Crole. "Go get her, precious. Scram!"

CHAPTER XV

CONVERGING PATHS

ESTHER ENTERED CROLE'S OFFICE looking hot and bothered. She dropped into a chair and said: "I've just about got time to make a report and get over to Judge Barnum's court for the noon recess."

"I'll be very attentive," said Crole.

"At six this morning I started to put in calls, one to Washington, and one to my friend's office in London. There is no record of Henry Brenan in the consul's office, or the office of the American Express. Nor was there any passport issued to Henry Brenan in Washington. He doesn't exist. It's my opinion that Gillespie arranged the sale through a dummy, selling it to himself."

"I suspected that much," sighed Crole. "Now I'm sure that the house deal was a phony."

Esther got up. "I had the calls charged to you."

"Fine," said Crole. "Send me your bill. I'll multiply it by two, and hope you can collect."

"I'll collect," promised Esther, flouncing out the door.

The girl had no more than left when Leahy appeared, looking somewhat crestfallen. "I guess," he began, sitting on the edge of the desk, "that we won't obtain possession of the secret file."

Crole's eyebrows moved up. "No?"

"No. I was down to the D.A.'s office all morning. And finally, on an excuse that the investigators had taken something of mine when they cleaned out Coughlin's desk, I got into the property room. There I found the list of things they were holding. But the memorandum book that Coughlin called his secret file was not amongst things. I searched pretty carefully. It wasn't there."

Crole gnawed on his lower lip. "Sure it was there in the first place?"

"Positive. I saw them put it in a box with some other things. While I was pawing around Minifie comes in and asks casually what it is I'm looking for. I told him nothing important—just a few notes on the horses that are scheduled to perform on the Santa Anita race track when the course opens."

"I think," said Crole, "that the D.A. has got the jump on us. He hasn't been bothering me all morning: When he's ignoring me I know he's got something in the way of a surprise—and a disagreeable one."

"What'll you do?"

"Nothing—as far as he's concerned. I've got other angles to be traced. Listen, Leahy, and I'll explain exactly how my agency stands in regard to these murders."

When he had finished, Leahy whistled softly. "It looks like your angles are beginning to point in a single direction. I've met Gillespie, but I never imagined him capable of anything like what's happened."

"One never knows. And with nearly a quarter of a million at stake, men can develop the characteristics of beasts who know no law but that of the jungle."

The telephone broke in harshly. Simon Crole regarded the instrument with dark suspicion, muttered beneath his breath, and took down the receiver. "Hello," he said.

"Mr. Crole?" asked a voice. "Listen. This is Scavillo."

Gene Selingo puffed heavily as he reached the county road following a steep climb from the canyon. Alone he had scrambled down its steep slope in search of Simon Crole's body. He had not found it, but he had found the .38 automatic that the agency man had snatched from his fingers a second before he went plunging out the car door. He had it now in the holster beneath his armpit.

The fact that he had been unable to discover Crole's body did not alarm him greatly. After all the canyon was a deep hole of a place, and he hadn't been any too thorough. The loss of the gun had worried him. But now that he had it safe in its holster once more, he shrugged off the remainder of the problem.

Ponderously he walked up the county road. Half a mile from the spot where he looked for the body, he saw a taxi drawn up beside the road. The driver was smoking a cigarette and seemed little concerned at sight of the big mobster striding along the road.

Selingo walked over to the cab and looked inside. "You're a long ways from the city, mister. Expect to pick up a fare?"

"Naw," shrugged Scavillo. "Just looking at the view. I always drive up here when I'm close by. A guy don't see views like this cruising around the city."

"What's in the view to look at?" Selingo wanted to know.

"I guess I'm simple. I like to look at the mountains."

"If you was to ask me, I'd say you was balmy. I think," he added ominously, "that you'd better move on. This is private property up here and we don't like to have the place jammed with people we don't know."

"Oke," said Scavillo. "I was just ready to leave when you came." The starter awoke the cab engine to life, and the taxi lurched down the county road.

Gene Selingo watched it until he could no longer see it, then turned, frowned, and kept going along the road until he reached a pair of iron gates anchored in columns of native rock.

Inside these gates, leaning against the stone-work, stood Ghost, a cigarette hanging loosely from his lips, hands thrust deep in his coat pockets.

"See anything of a cab around the place?" asked Selingo.

Mokund shook his head. "Ummm!"

"Geez," spat Selingo, "what a hole I've been in. But I found my rod. And was I relieved."

Together they walked up a gravel drive that circled widely through lanes of cypress and eucalyptus trees.

Beyond them was a rambling, spacious structure of wood and stone—the home of Ned Anderson.

They passed the caretaker, a beetle-browed Mexican who was clipping a hedge. They circled the house, went past a tennis court, an empty swimming pool, and by this circuitous route reached the service entrance to the kitchen.

In the kitchen itself they saw a dark-visaged man, another Mexican, fixing a panful of potatoes. He whittled the potatoes with a glittering, straight-bladed knife, instead of peeling them. On a shelf was a stack of fresh-made tortillas. To Selingo, they looked like stale, thin pancakes.

Over a range, heated with large wood chunks, hovered a fat round-bodied woman, with shiny black hair plastered tightly to her spherical head. Her face bore a striking resemblance to the stack of tortillas, and there were tiny globules of sweat on her forehead.

Through the kitchen wandered the two mobsters from the east. Past a butler's pantry into a breakfast room. Past this into a sun room. Then up a curved flight of stairs into a hall of confusing angles.

Selingo stopped at a certain door, moistened his lips and pushed it open. There were twin beds in the room. Ned Anderson was roped to one of them; Virginia Laird to the other. The eyes of Virginia were frightened. She turned her head on the pillow so she could look towards Anderson.

He saw the movement and smiled. Reassured, she closed her eyes to shut out the vision of these horrible men.

"Eeeeeeah!" yawned Mokund.

"It won't be long now," said Selingo, significantly. "Soon's the big guy gets back we'll start talking business."

They closed the door, strolled farther along the twisting hall and reached the door of another room. They pushed through. Seated in a chair near a desk was a pale and very frightened man. He was reading a newspaper that said among other things that he had been cleverly but foully murdered. That, of course, was not what frightened him. He had been prepared to read of his own death, but he was shocked almost into a paralysis to read of Coughlin's murder.

What had at first seemed amazingly simple was no longer simple. Complications had sprouted like octopus arms. There seemed to be no end to the mess in which he was involved. Anderson's death might have helped. But that blundering private detective had interfered. Thank God *he* was eliminated—a broken body in the deep fastness of Los Gatos canyon. He'd remain there for years without being discovered. A few hours more and he'd be away from all these complications, and with wealth enough to last him the rest of his years on earth.

He must pull himself together, regain his courage. He stared coldly at the mobsters in the doorway. "What is it?" he asked.

"Nothing," said Selingo. "Just looking the place over."

"You'd better stay outside and watch the road."

Selingo smirked cunningly. "Okay. Come on, Ghost. From the way things feel, I'd think we'd better look our bus over. No telling when we'll have to start back east."

Back they went through the crooked hall, down the stairs, through breakfast room, butler's pantry and kitchen. The fat, round-bodied woman was still sweating over the stove. But the Mexican who had been whittling potatoes was no longer in the kitchen.

Gene Selingo noted his absence, but not particularly. His mind was on the sleek, red car in the garage back of the house. Ghost Mokund, his face a blank, trailed alongside the larger man. Occasionally he sniffled, and an uneasy look flicked momentarily in his glassy eyes.

George Baron, immaculately attired, glanced with approving eyes at his packed bags. The east was calling him. And he was leaving the coastal city without a qualm. His home was in order. He was traveling light. Things could be replaced.

"Coughlin," he thought, "was right about Simon Crole. The private dick was too damned smart. But all that is over with. Brains aren't of any use in the skull of a dead man."

He looked at his watch. Examined his reflection in the mirror and was pleased with his appearance. He recalled, pleasurably, that he had things well in hand. Anderson and the girl were where the police couldn't reach them. The mobsters were watching things. Gillespie would get the cash out of hiding. And it would be divided impartially, dollar for dollar.

A hard glitter came into George Baron's eyes. He was not accustomed to dividing things with other men. He didn't intend to now. The risk had been too great and would continue to be great until Gillespie had passed the talking stage. His hand felt for the reassuring bulge in his hip pocket, then suddenly stiffened as a knock sounded on the door.

"What is it?" asked Baron, without moving.

"Mr. Baron," came the voice of the houseboy. "There's a man outside to see you. His name is Daniels."

The hard glitter returned to George Baron's eyes. Daniels, ace investigator for the District Attorney's office. What could he want? What did it matter what he wanted? It was bound to be serious. There had been a slip-up somewhere. Perhaps nothing important, but important enough to warrant Daniels coming to his apartment.

"Bring him in," he called.

Without undue signs of haste he carried his bags from the living room to the top of the back service stairs. Stopping in his bedroom he took a lounging robe from a hanger, fastened it around him, removed his hat, and went direct to the bathroom. Making certain that the drain in the tub was open, he opened both cold and hot water faucets. Then, with the collar of the robe held tight around his neck, he took a position close to the door and opened it only wide enough to display his head and shoulders.

Daniels came through the hall door and into the room. George Baron greeted him cheerfully from the bathroom doorway. "Just cleaning up a little, Daniels. Have a chair. Be with you in five minutes." Carefully he inched the door shut.

The investigator took out a package of cigarettes, lighted one and leaned comfortably back in Baron's most comfortable chair. There was a smug, satisfied look on his face—the same sort of an expression his face had worn when he had erred in thinking he had a perfect case against Simon Crole.

The minutes passed. Water ran in the bathroom in a torrent. Baron was making a good job of cleaning up. The cigarette burned itself up. Daniels lighted another one. More minutes passed. He began to twitch uneasily as he glared towards the closed door.

Finally, he got up, crossed the room and knocked. No answer. He opened the door. A shower of steam swirled into his face. He shouldered through it, shut off the water, and waited for the room to clear. He saw, then, that it was empty. There was a door leading to Baron's room. He passed through it and arrived at the back service stairs. But there was no sign of George Baron. He had quietly slipped away.

Daniels clomped back into the living room and called his superior on the phone.

"Someone must have warned him," said Minifie. "But that's all right. We'll get to him through someone else. Go over to Simon Crole's office and bring him in. Use any excuse you want to. And if you see Leahy, bring him in too. I haven't any doubt but what he's gone over to Crole's side. Crole's good at bribing. Once we get them down here, we'll start sweating them. I'm eternally weary of being made a fool of by that private dick. Get rough if you want to. But bring him in."

Daniels slammed out of the house. Dark clouds hung low in the sky. Sudden gusts of wind picked up dust and torn paper, whirling it around street comers. He drove downtown and parked. Hurried into the building where Crole had his office and crowded into an elevator.

Simon Crole, his hat on the back of his head, stood by his secretary's desk looking at his watch. "Precious," he said. "One of the men who made things unpleasant for me last night was seen by Scavillo. I'm sure of it. And where he is, there I'll find the other. Maybe they're all there." His eyes clouded. "If I take a gun, I'll be laying myself open for trouble. If I don't take one . . . hmmm! I wish Leahy would get back. Every second is important . . ."

The hall door opened suddenly. Investigator Daniels stood in the opening. "Going somewhere?" he asked in a voice mildly sarcastic.

"I thought I would," said Crole.

"Right. You're coming with me—to the D.A's office. Leahy here?" He looked through the open door into Crole's private office.

"I sent him away on important business," said Crole.

Daniels thrust the hall door shut with his heel. "I can find him later. But you're coming with me—now!"

"Yeah?"

"A-hunh! In case it hasn't as yet penetrated your thick skull there are still such things as material witness, obstruction of justice, and malfeasance. You're facing all of them."

"I'm in a hurry, Daniels," said Crole, evenly. "Will you please get the hell out of here and leave me alone. Your office hasn't a thing on me. Never has. And I'm warning you now that if you interfere with me you're going to regret it."

Daniels became mildly abusive. "Why you cheap dick. You can't get away with it this time. We're plenty wise to your methods. Taking money from both sides always has its kickback. And before our office is through with you, you'll wish you'd taken up some other profession."

"Stupidity," mused Crole. "How many errors are committed in thy name. Daniels, unless you've got a warrant for my arrest . . ."

He stopped. The hall door back of the investigator was opening. Leahy was coming in. Crole knotted his fist and cupped it in the palm of his left hand.

"Well if here isn't George Baron," he grinned.

Daniels whirled. Crole hit him then. Daniels staggered, recovered, and reached for his gun. Crole hit him again—a crushing hook to the jaw. Daniel's groaned, his eyes turned glassy. Sighing, he collapsed.

Etta stuffed a handkerchief into her mouth to muffle an involuntary scream. "Take it easy, precious," soothed Crole. "I didn't want to do it. But I've got to get out of here. The lives of several people are involved. He'll be all right in five minutes."

He faced Leahy. "Did you get anything?"

"Yeah, it's all down in the car packed in a suitcase."

"Good. I guess we're already to leave. All right. Let's get out of here before investigator Daniels comes out of the fog."

Though neither man knew it, the paths of Simon Crole and George Baron were rapidly converging upon a central point.

But Crole, his eyes half closed as he slouched on the back seat of Scavillo's cab, knew one thing—and knew it rather well. If his hunch proved wrong and bounced back in his face, District Attorney Minifie would be in a position to carry out his threat—which would mean the loss of his agency. Minifie had cherished the thought for so long a time that it had become an obsession with the man.

Crole started to roll a cigarette. The bouncing cab spilled his tobacco. Leahy produced a pack of tailor mades. Crole took one, lighted it and stared out the cab window.

There sure was going to be a storm—the first of the season. About time. Moisture was already forming on the windshield. Scavillo turned on the wiper.

The cab careened drunkenly through traffic and finally reached a four-lane boulevard. The lanes soon became stretches of smooth glistening cement. The cab slowed for an intersection, went beyond it and turned up the familiar county road.

"Go beyond the house," ordered Crole. "We'll walk back to it."

They got out beneath the shelter of trees close to a wire fence.

"Want me to stick around?" asked Scavillo.

"Yeah," nodded Crole, turning up his coat collar against the rain. "I think you'd better."

Crole led the way. They found a gate, passed through. The wind was tossing the flat, pointed leaves of the eucalyptus trees against the rain. Beyond the trees loomed the rambling house, gaunt, dripping. Occasionally a thin curl of smoke spewed from a chimney at the back of the house only to be whipped into nothingness as the wind pounced upon it.

The two men stood still, watching, listening. Trying to find some evidence of life. A man came out of a small building in the rear of the main house. He looked back over his shoulder as if fearful of what might be following him.

Crole raised his voice. "José!"

Hernandez whirled and came trotting through shrubs. He looked different without his chocolate colored suit. Relief was on his face as he stopped before the agency man.

"Mr. Crole, I am so glad you have arrived. They are here. Many are here in this grand house. Two are tied with ropes. With my own eyes have I seen them."

"Man and woman?"

"Yes. And a third has a room to himself where he broods. He is not a happy man." He pointed at a tall jacaranda tree. "The windows of that room are close to that tree."

"Anybody else, José?"

José Hernandez reverted to type. *"Nombre de Dios!* They are an evil pair. They move all over. Never are they quiet."

Crole turned to Leahy. "Couple of imported mobsters." Then speaking to Hernandez. "Where are they now?"

José shrugged. "I do not know. I avoid them. To protect myself I have only this." He displayed the knife with which he had whittled potatoes.

"It looks like a good knife," said Crole.

Hernandez wiped the wet blade on his pants. "With it," he said, without any trace of boasting, "I once killed a bandit in my country."

"That's fine, José. But get it out of sight. You won't need it here. Your next problem is to get us into the house without anyone seeing us."

Hernandez nodded and led them through an ivy-covered cellar entrance. They followed him closely.

There was an anxious look in the agency man's eyes as he turned to Leahy. "The contents of that suitcase. Are you sure you can . . .?"

"Leave the job to me, Simon. I've had experience. It ought to work, providing . . ."

"Sure, providing we're lucky. And Leahy. Once you get the things in proper shape, I want you to slip into the room Hernandez will point out. In it are two people. One is my client, Anderson. The second is Gillespie's secretary. Take them out of the house to Scavillo's cab and send them to my office. Ride with them as far as the nearest phone on the main highway and put in a rush call for Captain Jorgens."

"You intend to stay here alone?"

"José will be with me. Do like I tell you, and don't worry."

Their voices became hushed as they crawled up the steps leading to the butler's pantry. As they emerged into a region of many shelves, Crole could hear the steady drumming of rain against a window. He was thankful for the outside disturbance. It would help to deaden the sound of their movements in the upper rooms and hall.

They climbed the stairs softly. The house was deathly quiet. There was no sound but the sigh of the wind and the swish of rain.

CHAPTER XVI

LOS GATOS CANYON

AS GEORGE BARON drove his car through swirls of rain along the curved drive in front of the rambling house, he saw that both Selingo and Mokund were standing in the shelter of the front porch roof.

He did not remove his bags. Simply turned off the ignition switch and walked with dignity up the front stairs where the two mobsters waited him.

"Everything all right?" he asked.

"Just swell, Mr. Baron. Couldn't be better," said Selingo. "You look like you're going places. I can see the bags on the back seat of your car. Things getting hot down below?"

"Very. But I'm not leaving till you boys are taken care of."

Ghost Mokund scratched a match on a porch column, lighted a cigarette and flicked the burning wood ember out into the rain. If he had any thoughts at all, they were sewed up tight in the back of his head.

Selingo said: "Just so as you don't fade, Baron, and leave us here in this lonesome spot. We aren't looking for trouble. And we aren't backing away from it. We got plenty coming, and . . ."

"Don't start anything," warned George Baron, "with me. I'm on my way to collect. When I return, you and Mokund will receive everything I promised you."

"Maybe I'd better go with you, Baron."

"It isn't necessary. Stay here where you can watch my car and the driveway—just in case."

"Sure," grinned Selingo. "But don't take too long. I want to scram out of this locality. It's beginning to get me. These mountains feel like they're pressing down on me."

Baron looked at his henchman sharply, shrugged and went inside.

James Gillespie tried to appear casual when George Baron entered the room. But it was hard to be casual when a fortune of two hundred thousand dollars is involved. He hadn't wholly trusted Baron when he made out that insurance policy. He didn't trust him now. The room felt suddenly hot. He went to a casement window and opened it. Wind and rain stung his cheeks.

George Baron said: "An investigator from the District Attorney's office came to my house. I don't know how they traced things to me. It's time we left the state." His voice was suave as usual. He might have been explaining a certain point of law to a doubtful judge.

"I was afraid something would happen." Gillespie's mouth and hands began to tremble.

"My car's outside," said Baron. "I'll take you with me to the air field." He looked at his watch. "There's a transport leaving for Chicago in three quarters of an hour. We can make it easy."

Gillespie knew, as he had known all along, that the moment he had dreaded had come—the division of cash and bonds. He swallowed heavily and tried by a feeble pretext to put off the inevitable.

"Is it necessary that we leave now—in this storm?"

"Quite. If that investigator traces me here, I'm afraid certain acts we have committed might prove a strong deterrent against our ever leaving the state."

James Gillespie nodded. And his smile was a weak lip movement. He took the cushion from the chair in which he had been sitting. Turned it over. The inner springs had been removed. In their place was a black leather bag with a zipper top.

"You selected a good place to conceal it," said Baron. "How much is there?"

Gillespie bent down and began to take out packages of currency and bonds. Baron crossed to the other man's side. Deliberately took the gun from his hip pocket, jammed it against Gillespie's side, and without a flicker of emotion in his suave face, pulled the trigger.

There followed a thick, muffled explosion, and a choking gasp.

Gillespie sagged forward to his knees, rocked back and forward. Cupped his face with hands that seemed to stiffen into claws, gasped a second time, and collapsed over on his side. One eye stared, Cyclopean like, through the V formed by two spread fingers. Reflected in that single eye was malevolence and intolerable pain.

George Baron, however, took no further notice of his victim. He knew exactly where he had placed that single bullet. He lifted the leather bag from the floor and set it on the desk for a closer inspection of its contents. Satisfied, he pulled the zipper shut and was about to step over Gillespie's body towards the door when he thought he heard a sound in the hall.

Indecision gripped him. His lips tightened. He took a firmer grip on the gun still held in his right hand. Then taking two steps backward he looked out the window towards the drive. Except for his own machine, the drive was wetly empty.

He pivoted suddenly, as if swung around by some unseen hand. Then froze into stark immobility as his eyes focused on the shadowy apparition of one whom he thought was dead. Standing in the opening was Simon Crole, water dripping from sodden garments. His eyes seemed abnormally large with accusation. And his lips were twisted crookedly. He looked surprised.

An errant gust of wind came walking through the casement window. Laid gusty hands on the door, and firmly closed it. The spell broken, George Baron raised his arm rapidly and fired five shots through the door panel at the exact spot at which the apparition should be standing.

Then, drawing in a deep breath, he leaped forward and jerked the door inwards. The hall was empty—that part of it which he could see. He could feel his heart pumping in a way it was not accustomed to as the valves opened and closed with irregular thuds.

He stood there with the prize gripped in one hand, a faintly smoking revolver in the other. His lips moved. "It can't be. I'm seeing things. I know. I'm nervous, jumpy. Must get control of myself. Must . . ."

He whirled again. Simon Crole was in the room, feet spread wide, staring at the body on the floor. When the wind had blown the door shut he had followed the crooked hall to a second door. He passed through this second opening just as Baron moved towards the hall.

Baron said: "You're not dead."

The surprised smile was still on the agency man's face. "Drop your gun, Baron. Everything's ended. There'll be no more murders."

"So? I admire your nerve, Crole. But it's not going to save you now. No man can stop me, even you, clever as you are."

"Words, Baron. You can't kill me like you did the others. Two of your hired mobsters tried it. Did it work? No. They lied to you, Baron. They lied because they weren't as proficient in their art as they thought they were. Two against one. And they both had guns. I was unarmed the same as I am now. And even *you* can't hurt me."

The eyes of the attorney became brittle. "I was warned against you, Simon Crole, by a man named Coughlin. I didn't heed his warning because I thought I had a better brain than you. I still think so."

"Whistling in the dark. That's what you're doing, Baron. With every beat of your heart you know that fear is getting you down. Put away your gun or drop it. Either way suits me. The police are on their way. Listen! Can't you hear the sirens?"

"No!" George Baron's eyes flashed. "Neither can you." He raised the gun till it was level with Crole's chest. "Selingo!" he screamed. "Get up here. Fast! Thought I was alone, eh? I'm not. Two good gunmen. You won't get past them a second time . . ."

Crole moved in. Baron leered unpleasantly and pulled the trigger. The gun clicked and kept on clicking as he frantically tried to make empty cartridges explode.

His eyes narrowed. He swung with the gun barrel and missed. Crole had him suddenly by the wrist. The attorney dropped the bag and struck wildly at the agency man. Crole hit him hard. Baron crashed against the wall, his hand pawing a bruised cheek.

His eyes forked lightning, his lips foul curses. They seemed out of place with one so extremely suave and sure of himself. But Baron was no longer a dignified attorney. Civilization had dropped from his shoulders. He was a criminal, a murderer—and a traitor to his own kind.

He rubbed his eyes to hide the molten hate he felt for this one man who stood between him and freedom. He was stalling for time, waiting for his two hired killers to come to his aid.

"I'll divide with you, Crole, evenly, dollar for dollar. You've got everything to gain. A hundred thousand dollars. Don't you see, man? It's a fortune—a fortune for each of us.

"Stop looking at me that way. Maybe I tried to kill you. Let it pass. We'll be friends, not enemies!" He strained his ears for footsteps in the hall. And all he could hear was the beat of rain and the sigh of the wind.

"I might have known," said Crole, coldly, "that you'd try to bribe me. But if I wanted that money, Baron, I'd take all of it. And you wouldn't stop me."

"You've got to listen to me, Crole. What will you gain by turning me over to the police? Glory? You know perfectly well that'll go to somebody else. Money? A small fee. You're no more honest than I am. I'm offering you a fortune just to step out of my way." Simon Crole was bending over Gillespie. "This man isn't dead," he said, "but it's no fault of yours, Baron." He shook his head slowly. "But whether he lives or dies, the answer is the same. You'll get the rope, and so will those . . ."

"Raise 'em, guy! Reach for the ceiling!" The command was ominous and came from behind.

Simon Crole lifted his hands slowly, his eyes slitting as he turned ever so slowly.

"Good," breathed Baron. "Keep him covered."

"What's the argument?" asked Selingo.

"Gillespie accidentally got in the way of a bullet from my gun," said Baron, his self-confidence returning in a flood. "Then this private detective came in through the door."

Selingo rubbed the stubble on his chin. "Move over against that panel next to the window, Ghost. This guy Crole is full of tricks. Let him have it in the belly if he starts anything. What's this talk I heard about a fortune being split?"

Baron moistened his lips. "Nothing that concerns you. Keep this man covered while I . . ."

"Oh no, Baron. You're slippery as Crole. I don't trust you either. What do you mean by a fortune? Me and Ghost take all the risks and maybe our share is a couple grand. Come clean."

"The fortune," Crole explained, "is over two hundred thousand dollars. Baron was entitled to half of it, Gillespie the other half. But Baron was a hog. He wanted it all. So he gets rid of Gillespie. Nice playmate you've got, Selingo."

"Yeah. Keep your lips buttoned up, Mister. I ain't forgot how you shoved that bald head of yours into my neck. And I still remember how you slugged me down at the hotel."

The eyes of the agency man ranged slowly from Mokund to Selingo, then came to rest on the baseboard behind the desk. He saw then what he looked for. Leahy was a good man. Damned good. By now he should be well on his way down the county road.

He wondered, idly, how long it would take the police to get here. And without realizing it, he found himself in the same position as Baron had been but a few seconds ago when time meant everything.

"Maybe I was a little rough with you, Selingo," he said, smoothly. "After all, you and your little pal had me on the spot—were going to bump me. I don't like to die any more than the next man."

"Kill him!" croaked Mokund.

"Don't rush things," said Crole. "There's no hurry as I can see. We're all alone on the mountain."

"You remarked about a siren a moment ago," drawled Baron.

"Bluff," said Crole. "How was I to reach the police?"

"I wonder. Did you come here alone?"

"Alone, Baron. On a hunch. Didn't expect to find so many people here. It was a great surprise."

"You're due for a still greater one, Crole."

"Like Gillespie, for example."

"It was necessary to remove him," nodded Baron. "He was in the way. And it's going to be necessary to remove you."

Crole wagged his head sadly. "It's going to be dangerous for you and your mobsters, Baron. Their description and that of their car is being broadcasted and teletyped all over the state."

"They'll never pin that on us," boasted Selingo.

"Won't they, though? Have you forgotten Coughlin?"

Baron shrugged. "His tongue was sealed the same as yours is going to be."

"You killed Coughlin, Baron?"

"I had no other alternative, Crole, any more than I have with you."

"Then you admit it," persisted Crole. "And you tried to frame it so that the blame would fall on me." George Baron bent and picked his gun from the floor. "I still don't see how you escaped a formal charge."

"You guys have palavered long enough," broke in Selingo. "One of us has got to bump him."

Crole said: "My arms are tired."

"Don't put 'em down," warned Selingo. "Maybe I'd better frisk you." He came close and patted the agency man's hips. Felt beneath the arms for a shoulder harness, and scowled. "Where's your rod?"

"I don't carry any."

"You mean you came here all alone—without no gun?"

"That's correct. I don't need any. Right now I've got something just as deadly. Going somewheres, Baron?"

Selingo's gun arm wavered as he flung a startled glance at the attorney gathering up the zipper bag.

Crole's right arm jerked downward. His elbow jammed Selingo's wrist, knocking the gun one side. It exploded harshly and the bullet went through the open casement window showering the carpet with glass.

Selingo howled as the edge of Crole's hand clipped his wrist. Sharp pain caused him to drop it. They fell on it together. The gun in Ghost Mokund's hand began to blast with sustained thunder.

George Baron faded, the zipper bag clutched tightly to his chest.

Crole wrapped his arms around Selingo's neck, and with his foot he kicked the gun across the room. Mokund came closer. He had to be careful not to shoot the wrong man.

"Blast him!" screamed Selingo. "He's killing me . . ."

Their twisting, surging bodies rolled towards Mokund. He hopped back, collided with the edge of the open casement window, lost his balance, recovered, and stood swaying.

Expressionless he watched the two men on the floor. Their strained, harsh breathing rasped against his ears. Crole's big body was now at the top of the heap. Mokund aimed his gun. Bodies twisted. Now Selingo was in the line of fire. Mokund wasn't a fast thinker. Nor was he over-endowed with physical courage except when the magic of the white powder coursed through his body.

He wished he had some now. His gun arm started to tremble as thought suggestion created a throbbing desire for the drug. Selingo screamed again. Then the sound was abruptly choked off as a bunched fist hit him in the mouth.

Mokund backed away warily. His body was against the wood paneling of the room. The craving was upon him. He fought against it. Instinctively he rubbed the back of his hand beneath his nostrils. Something like an animal-like whine pushed his lips open.

His eyes left the combatants on the floor, swerved slowly and came to rest on a dark-faced man standing in the hall. Comprehension dawned slowly. Here was someone to kill.

He could kill all right if there wasn't anything in the way. He was a good killer—with a gun.

The trembling went out of his arm. He lifted it for a snap shot. His eyes paled, became icy. "Ummm!" he grunted, his gun arm starting to move down.

But the downward movement started a split second too late. The arm of the man in the hall whipped forward like a striking snake. A single steel fang shot out, hissed sharply. And the blade of the thrown knife buried itself in Mokund's wrist.

He cried out sharply. The gun slipped from nerveless fingers, and he stared with shocked, protruding eyes at the bright thing in his bleeding wrist.

José Hernandez jumped into the room. He picked up Mokund's gun. Without any hesitation he gripped its barrel and brought it down with a resounding thock on Gene Selingo's head.

The man groaned and went limp. Crole got to his feet, breathing heavily. He looked curiously at Mokund writhing on the floor with the point of a knife sticking through his wrist.

"José," he said, admiringly, "thanks. You get better all the time. How much was it I promised you for this day's work?"

"The amount was thirty-five dollars aside from the freedom of a debt to you of ten. That was our agreement."

Crole picked up Selingo's automatic, thought of something, and leaned close as he whispered into Hernandez's ear. "Ten times that amount, José. That's what you will be paid. You have my promise. Now please go down below. I think I hear a car out on the drive. But give me the little man's gun before you go. Fine!"

CHAPTER XVII

VOICES OF THE DEAD

GEORGE BARON HAD EVERYTHING to be thankful for. Currency, bonds. The prize was intact, and he hadn't had to share the fortune with anybody. He realized that he couldn't have arranged it better.

No need to worry over the mobsters from the east. Crole was as good as dead right now. Then Selingo and Mokund, though aware that he had abandoned them, would immediately get out of the state.

He had had a close call—two in fact. But his quick thinking had enabled him to avoid both traps. He smiled pleasurably at his own astuteness as he guided the car down the long grade to the main highway.

It loomed before him now, just beyond a red-diamond sign which read: STOP.

He stopped and his eyes narrowed for he had seen two blue uniforms in a car that was turning onto the county road. He pretended not to notice the car, shifted into second gear and sent his machine hurtling into the outer lane of north bound traffic towards the not too distant airport.

Leahy, riding with the driver in the police car, turned in the seat. "Captain, stop that car! Baron's in it. He'll get away!"

The police car trembled to a stop. Jorgens leaped out. Two motorcycle patrolmen had been following the police machine. The captain flagged them to a stop and pointed at Baron's disappearing machine. "Arrest the driver of that car. Bring him to headquarters, car and all. Never mind if he squawks. If it's a false arrest, Leahy, believe me I'll take it out of Simon Crole's hide. Up the hill, driver," he ordered, climbing back into the machine. "Damn this rain!"

José Hernandez, polite and slightly nervous of the blue uniforms, led Captain Jorgens and Sergeant Breen into the room of death. Simon Crole sat hunched in a chair, a gun in each hand. The mobsters were sitting with their backs to the wall. Selingo was glaring his hate. Mokund was sniffling as he stared at the handkerchief Crole had used to bind his wounded wrist.

"Well?" rumbled Jorgens, his eyes darting bird-like from the corpse on the floor, to the other two men, then back to Simon Crole in the chair. "Don't tell me, Simon, that there's been another murder."

Crole pursed his lips and nodded slowly. "That's the way it is, Captain. And the killer got away—an attorney named Baron."

"We passed his car at the foot of the hill," said Jorgens, "and I sent two highway patrol officers to bring him to headquarters."

"Fast thinking, Captain, for you."

"Blame Leahy. Who's the stiff?"

"James Gillespie."

"Oh hell," raged the police captain. "Him again."

"He's been murdered a second time, Captain. This time for good. Once when his car went over Iron Mountain into the canyon, and now with a bullet from George Baron's gun snuggling close to his heart."

"There's going to be an unholy row about this in the papers, Simon."

"There'd be a worse row, Captain, if everything wasn't solved. I wish you could have gotten here sooner to hear Gillespie's last words, but it really won't make much difference."

"What might that mean?"

"Oh, several things of an important nature concerning my client—and me."

"You?"

"Yeah, me. Simon gets a break, Captain. A swell confession."

Jorgens shrugged and turned to Breen. "Send the driver down to the nearest phone and get word to the medical examiner. We can't do anything till he looks at the body."

"If you'll just keep an eye on these two hoods," said Crole, yawning and rising to his feet, "I'll be going home. You should be able to handle it without me."

"All right. But remain near your phone until . . ."

"I won't be going anywheres, Captain. My work's about done, except collecting my fees."

"Fees!" scoffed Jorgens. "Cripes, don't you ever think of anything but how much you can bleed from your clients?"

"Bleed is not the right word, Captain. My clients always give me what they think I deserve. A sort of an elastic arrangement, but it always works out swell for everybody concerned." He rubbed his nose for a moment and said: "The red car belonging to these mobsters is in the garage. Thought you ought to know." Selingo's mouth spewed a vile epithet.

Crole sighed. "You boys should have stayed in the east and away from our city. Coming out here was just too bad. Be seeing you, Captain."

He inclined his head towards Leahy. Together they went out into the crooked hall. "Get possession of the necessary things," he ordered. "We'll leave the rest for the D.A.'s men to gather up."

Leahy disappeared and came back in a few moments with something wrapped in a towel. "All set," he said, "but how are we going to get back to town?"

"Scavillo will be somewhere outside," said Crole, trustingly.

And the cab driver was there, waiting in the rain.

They were gathered together in the District Attorney's office, a dripping, sullen and slightly puzzled group of men.

District Attorney Minifie sat grimly behind his desk, his tired eyes straining in an effort to look into every face at once. Selingo and Mokund were sullen. Linked with steel cuffs, all their bravado was gone. Mokund was still sniffling.

Breen and Captain Jorgens were the puzzled ones. Leahy, his face registering nothing in particular, stared at the dirt under his finger nails. And Simon Crole alone seemed to be the only pleasant spirit in the room.

"Anderson," Minifie was saying, "has told a somewhat incomplete story. Miss Laird's is equally incoherent. Coughlin is dead. But he left behind a small book filled with cryptic notations. These notes seem to indicate, Crole, that he feared you for some reason not quite clear. I'm afraid I'll have to hold you pending further investigation."

"So you had the book all the time, eh?" smiled Crole.

"All the time. Perhaps you'll explain at this hearing why you murdered Coughlin."

Crole said patiently: "Coughlin was shot by George Baron."

Minifie's lips tightened. He shot a sudden question at Gene Selingo. "Was Baron the man who shot . . .?"

"How the hell should I know!" snarled Selingo.

"Your machine forced Gillespie's over the hill. Don't lie now."

"I ain't talking."

The phone rang sharply. Minifie took down the receiver. "Office of the District Attorney," he said. He listened for a moment then set the receiver on the desk. "Yours, Captain Jorgens."

The captain placed the receiver near his ear. "Yeah?" he said.

The voice over the wire was clearly audible. "We arrested Baron, but he got nasty and hauled out a gun. We afterwards found out that the rod was empty. But by that time a slug from O'rourke's .38 special went through his head. He squawked once, then quieted down. He's been quiet ever since."

"You mean he died?" snapped Jorgens, petulantly.

"That's right," said the voice. "We have his body in his own car in front of headquarters. What shall we do?"

Simon Crole, hearing distinctly the officer's report, said: "Tell him, Captain, to pay special attention to a bag with a zipper top. It's filled with money and bonds that are the property of my client, Ned Anderson."

"Keep a couple of men guarding the machine and everything that's in it," ordered Jorgens. "I'll be over in a few minutes. Let anything disappear from that car and someone will have to answer to me personally." He hung up rather violently.

District Attorney Minifie, who had also heard the voice, said: "George Baron dead, Gillespie ditto, Coughlin the same. No one left but these two gangsters, and they won't talk. It looks like things are going to be even more difficult to explain, Crole."

"Mind if I smoke, Mister District Attorney?"

"Why should I, if it will help your thinking."

"My thinking is all done—and finished with." He rolled a flat cigarette and puffed contentedly.

"Perhaps you can explain your unwarranted attack on one of the investigators this afternoon. Smoke two cigarettes, Crole. You'll need them."

"One's quite enough," said Crole, drily. "And it's time I was getting back to my office. Leahy, if you've got that evidence with you, I wish you would place it on the District Attorney's desk."

"Evidence?" Minifie's voice was almost a whisper. "Whose?"

"You ought to know your own property when you see it, Minifie. It's the detectaphone outfit you had a man install in my apartment. It didn't work out so well. The man who installed it was so stupid as to disturb a favorite picture of mine. I guessed what was behind that picture right away."

Minifie's eyes began to grow sad.

"So," Crole continued, "since everything was still in my apartment this afternoon, I sent Leahy over after it. We were going to a house that formerly belonged to my client, and I reckoned it might be a nice toy to take along with us."

He paused, inhaled, and smiled. "We took it. Leahy wired it through a hall to the right room. And everything said in that room is down on this nice black disk. You will hear my voice, Baron's, and the yammerings of his hired killers. But best of all, Mister District Attorney, you'll hear the final confession of James Gillespie, the man who was murdered twice. I had to bring the tiny microphone close to his lips. But he managed to whisper most of the details of his embezzlement before his voice choked up."

"I see," said Minifie, collapsing tiredly, his head leaning against the back of his chair. "Evidence of that kind, taken in that manner, is acceptable to me, Crole."

"I was quite certain it would be."

"You can go, Crole. The longer I look at your face, the sicker I get. The wax record, of course, will remain the property of my office."

"Of course, since it was yours in the first place. No bad feelings, I hope."

"Yes," sighed Minifie. "But I'll get over them soon enough."

Simon Crole smiled again, signaled to Leahy, and together both men left the prosecutor's office.

On the way to his own office Crole said to Leahy: "You did an excellent job. Want your money now?"

"Any time," said Leahy.

"Come down in the morning, and your check will be ready."

"Oke," said Leahy. "I'll be there—early."

When he reached his office he found it crowded. It was late. But Etta was still behind her desk, valiantly waiting. He patted her shoulder on the way in. "Everything's over, precious. You can call it a day and go home. If you feel like celebrating, I'd suggest a new fur coat. Winter's coming, and there's gonna be plenty of rainy days. But no more than two hundred bucks, precious. If it's a nickel more than that, I'll make you send it back."

He was always doing nice things like that. It made the moisture jump to the back of her eyes. She pressed two fingers on her lips, touched them lightly to his cheek and said: "You're swell, boss."

Blushing, Simon Crole went into his own office and there found Ned Anderson, Virginia Laird, and—once more clad in a chocolate-brown suit—José Hernandez.

"José," he said, "the banks are closed!"

"That's all right, Señor Crole. I will come in the morning. As you said, ten times the amount you promised me. That is a sum I cannot reckon without paper and pencil."

"Three hundred and fifty dollars," boomed Crole. "Be down early." He pressed the Mexican's hand. "You saved my life, José. Even when I have paid you, I'll still be in your debt."

"There is yet Manuel," said Hernandez.

"Yes, Manuel. But believe me, José, the next time he needs to be set on the straight and narrow road, I'll attend to it personally."

José Hernandez left, beaming.

Crole turned to his client. "Well?"

"Is it all over, Simon?" asked Anderson.

"Practically, and you'll get back every cent that Gillespie had of yours up to the moment he was killed. It may take a few days, but it won't have to go through the courts."

He turned to Virginia Laird. "You have gone through a somewhat disagreeable experience, my dear. And I admire your courage in coming to Anderson in the first place. What made you do it?"

"I really don't know," said the girl, softly.

"And she lost her job," said Anderson, "because of me. I asked her to marry me once. She said 'don't be silly.' Tonight, when I am again a guest at the Commodore, I'll ask her again."

Virginia Laird smiled at the agency man. "What would *you* do?"

"Accept him, my dear, and congratulations to the both of you." He extended his hands.

"Make out your bill for services, Simon," said Anderson, "and . . ."

Crole led them to the hall door. "Come in tomorrow, and we'll talk everything over."

"We'll be here," nodded Anderson. "Good night, Simon."

Crole's smile was heavy with fatigue. "Good night, my friends."

The office quieted. Crole dropped into the chair behind his desk. There was a commotion in the hall but he paid no attention to it. His mind was on his comforting bottle of Bourbon. He stood it on the desk.

In came Matt Ridley, wet and flushed. "Am I in time, boss? Did I do good work on the Smith angle?"

"Couldn't be better, Matt. And the case is closed."

"Gosh! So soon? And me not in at the finish."

"I had other help. Capable men, too." He poured two liberal glasses of the Bourbon, and smacked his lips with anticipatory cluckings. Sighed, and reached for the last glass in the drawer. Through the door came Captain Jorgens—dour as usual.

Crole filled the third glass, and darkly surveyed what remained in the bottle.

"I'm glad to see you again, Captain. Is everything all right at police headquarters?"

Jorgens savored the Bourbon. "Things are in a mess. Two fresh bodies on the morgue slabs. Otherwise everything is all right."

"Minifie was slightly annoyed when he sent me away. Has he gotten over his grouch?"

"After hearing what was on that wax record he couldn't very well do anything else. But he was having a grand time with the reporters when I left. There'll be extras pouring from the presses before the next couple of hours."

Simon Crole drank slowly, enjoying the flavor. After a moment he said: "You did not come here, Captain, just on the off chance of getting a drink. Suppose we clean up the last point, if there is still one left."

"There is," said Jorgens. "Among the papers we picked up in Gillespie's office there was a will and an insurance policy." He glanced at Crole sharply. "Did you know about either of them?"

"Slightly," nodded Crole. "I checked the insurance policy for possible motivation, and drew a blank." Jorgens took a cigar from his pocket, eyed it speculatively and thrust it between his teeth. "Have you collected from your client yet?"

"Not yet," sighed Crole. "I was too tired to be bothered right now. The fee will be exceedingly large."

"That I can well believe if the client is rich. But you must know already that there was something unusual in Gillespie's policy. And that the beneficiary was to be selected according to the terms of the will."

"I knew that," nodded Crole.

"But did you know that Gillespie never thoroughly trusted George Baron; that he went into this scheme of embezzlement against his will and at the instigation of Baron."

"That I surmised."

"But did you surmise what that particular clause in the will was?"

"No. I was and still am—quite ignorant."

"I'm glad you'll admit it. Listen. When Gillespie took out that policy he did it with but one purpose in mind. He wanted somebody to square his account—just in case he was accidentally or otherwise killed. And to the person who turned up his killer goes the face value of the policy—Twenty-five thousand dollars." Simon Crole sat very still letting this choice morsel circulate through his mental mechanism. Finally he said: "Then I collect from the insurance company. That it?"

"Yes," choked Jorgens. "Can you match that for luck?"

The lips of the private detective twitched and formed themselves in their usual surprised smile. He wagged his head solemnly. "No, Captain, I can't match it. I don't believe I'd care to try." He rubbed his hands, blinked, and said solemnly: "Another drink, Captain Jorgens?"

RAMBLE HOUSE's

HARRY STEPHEN KEELER WEBWORK MYSTERIES

(RH) indicates the title is available ONLY in the RAMBLE HOUSE edition

The Ace of Spades Murder
The Affair of the Bottled Deuce (RH)
The Amazing Web
The Barking Clock
Behind That Mask
The Book with the Orange Leaves
The Bottle with the Green Wax Seal
The Box from Japan
The Case of the Canny Killer
The Case of the Crazy Corpse (RH)
The Case of the Flying Hands (RH)
The Case of the Ivory Arrow
The Case of the Jeweled Ragpicker
The Case of the Lavender Gripsack
The Case of the Mysterious Moll
The Case of the 16 Beans
The Case of the Transparent Nude (RH)
The Case of the Transposed Legs
The Case of the Two-Headed Idiot (RH)
The Case of the Two Strange Ladies
The Circus Stealers (RH)
Cleopatra's Tears
A Copy of Beowulf (RH)
The Crimson Cube (RH)
The Face of the Man From Saturn
Find the Clock
The Five Silver Buddhas
The 4th King
The Gallows Waits, My Lord! (RH)
The Green Jade Hand
Finger! Finger!
Hangman's Nights (RH)
I, Chameleon (RH)
I Killed Lincoln at 10:13! (RH)
The Iron Ring
The Man Who Changed His Skin (RH)
The Man with the Crimson Box
The Man with the Magic Eardrums
The Man with the Wooden Spectacles
The Marceau Case
The Matilda Hunter Murder

The Monocled Monster
The Murder of London Lew
The Murdered Mathematician
The Mysterious Card (RH)
The Mysterious Ivory Ball of Wong Shing Li (RH)
The Mystery of the Fiddling Cracksman
The Peacock Fan
The Photo of Lady X (RH)
The Portrait of Jirjohn Cobb
Report on Vanessa Hewstone (RH)
Riddle of the Travelling Skull
Riddle of the Wooden Parrakeet (RH)
The Scarlet Mummy (RH)
The Search for X-Y-Z
The Sharkskin Book
Sing Sing Nights
The Six From Nowhere (RH)
The Skull of the Waltzing Clown
The Spectacles of Mr. Cagliostro
Stand By—London Calling!
The Steeltown Strangler
The Stolen Gravestone (RH)
Strange Journey (RH)
The Strange Will
The Straw Hat Murders (RH)
The Street of 1000 Eyes (RH)
Thieves' Nights
Three Novellos (RH)
The Tiger Snake
The Trap (RH)
Vagabond Nights (Defrauded Yeggman)
Vagabond Nights 2 (10 Hours)
The Vanishing Gold Truck
The Voice of the Seven Sparrows
The Washington Square Enigma
When Thief Meets Thief
The White Circle (RH)
The Wonderful Scheme of Mr. Christopher Thorne
X. Jones—of Scotland Yard
Y. Cheung, Business Detective

Keeler Related Works

A To Izzard: A Harry Stephen Keeler Companion by Fender Tucker — Articles and stories about Harry, by Harry, and in his style. Included is a compleat bibliography.

Wild About Harry: Reviews of Keeler Novels — Edited by Richard Polt & Fender Tucker — 22 reviews of works by Harry Stephen Keeler from *Keeler News*. A perfect introduction to the author.

The Keeler Keyhole Collection: Annotated newsletter rants from Harry Stephen Keeler, edited by Francis M. Nevins. Over 400 pages of incredibly personal Keeleriana.

Fakealoo — Pastiches of the style of Harry Stephen Keeler by selected demented members of the HSK Society. Updated every year with the new winner.

Strands of the Web: Short Stories of Harry Stephen Keeler — 29 stories, just about all that Keeler wrote, are edited and introduced by Fred Cleaver.

RAMBLE HOUSE's LOON SANCTUARY

A Clear Path to Cross — Sharon Knowles short mystery stories by Ed Lynskey.

A Corpse Walks in Brooklyn and Other Stories — Volume 5 in the Day Keene in the Detective Pulps series.

A Jimmy Starr Omnibus — Three 40s novels by Jimmy Starr.

A Niche in Time and Other Stories — Classic SF by William F. Temple

A Roland Daniel Double: The Signal and The Return of Wu Fang — Classic thrillers from the 30s.

A Shot Rang Out — Three decades of reviews and articles by today's Anthony Boucher, Jon Breen. An essential book for any mystery lover's library.

A Smell of Smoke — A 1951 English countryside thriller by Miles Burton.

A Snark Selection — Lewis Carroll's *The Hunting of the Snark* with two Snarkian chapters by Harry Stephen Keeler — Illustrated by Gavin L. O'Keefe.

A Young Man's Heart — A forgotten early classic by Cornell Woolrich.

Alexander Laing Novels — *The Motives of Nicholas Holtz* and *Dr. Scarlett*, stories of medical mayhem and intrigue from the 30s.

An Angel in the Street — Modern hardboiled noir by Peter Genovese.

Automaton — Brilliant treatise on robotics: 1928-style! By H. Stafford Hatfield.

Away From the Here and Now — Clare Winger Harris stories, collected by Richard A. Lupoff

Beast or Man? — A 1930 novel of racism and horror by Sean M'Guire. Introduced by John Pelan.

Black Beadle — A 1939 thriller by E.C.R. Lorac.

Black Hogan Strikes Again — Australia's Peter Renwick pens a tale of the 30s outback.

Black River Falls — Suspense from the master, Ed Gorman.

Blondy's Boy Friend — A snappy 1930 story by Philip Wylie, writing as Leatrice Homesley.

Blood in a Snap — The *Finnegan's Wake* of the 21st century, by Jim Weiler.

Blood Moon — The first of the Robert Payne series by Ed Gorman.

Bogart '48 — Hollywood action with Bogie by John Stanley and Kenn Davis

Calling Lou Largo! — Two Lou Largo novels by William Ard.

Cornucopia of Crime — Francis M. Nevins assembled this huge collection of his writings about crime literature and the people who write it. Essential for any serious mystery library.

Corpse Without Flesh — Strange novel of forensics by George Bruce

Crimson Clown Novels — By Johnston McCulley, author of the Zorro novels, *The Crimson Clown* and *The Crimson Clown Again*.

Dago Red — 22 tales of dark suspense by Bill Pronzini.

Dark Sanctuary — Weird Menace story by H. B. Gregory

David Hume Novels — *Corpses Never Argue, Cemetery First Stop, Make Way for the Mourners, Eternity Here I Come*. 1930s British hardboiled fiction with an attitude.

Dead Man Talks Too Much — Hollywood boozer by Weed Dickenson.

Death Leaves No Card — One of the most unusual murdered-in-the-tub mysteries you'll ever read. By Miles Burton.

Death March of the Dancing Dolls and Other Stories — Volume Three in the Day Keene in the Detective Pulps series. Introduced by Bill Crider.

Deep Space and other Stories — A collection of SF gems by Richard A. Lupoff.

Detective Duff Unravels It — Episodic mysteries by Harvey O'Higgins.

Diabolic Candelabra — Classic 30s mystery by E.R. Punshon.

Dictator's Way — Another D.S. Bobby Owen mystery from E.R. Punshon

Dime Novels: Ramble House's 10-Cent Books — *Knife in the Dark* by Robert Leslie Bellem, *Hot Lead* and *Song of Death* by Ed Earl Repp, *A Hashish House in New York* by H.H. Kane, and five more.

Doctor Arnoldi — Tiffany Thayer's story of the death of death.

Don Diablo: Book of a Lost Film — Two-volume treatment of a western by Paul Landres, with diagrams. Intro by Francis M. Nevins.

Dope and Swastikas — Two strange novels from 1922 by Edmund Snell

Dope Tales #1 — Two dope-riddled classics; *Dope Runners* by Gerald Grantham and *Death Takes the Joystick* by Phillip Condé.

Dope Tales #2 — Two more narco-classics; *The Invisible Hand* by Rex Dark and *The Smokers of Hashish* by Norman Berrow.

Dope Tales #3 — Two enchanting novels of opium by the master, Sax Rohmer. *Dope* and *The Yellow Claw*.

Double Hot — Two 60s softcore sex novels by Morris Hershman.

Double Sex — Yet two more panting thrillers from Morris Hershman.

Dr. Odin — Douglas Newton's 1933 racial potboiler comes back to life.

Evangelical Cockroach — Jack Woodford writes about writing.

Evidence in Blue — 1938 mystery by E. Charles Vivian.

Fatal Accident — Murder by automobile, a 1936 mystery by Cecil M. Wills.

Fighting Mad — Todd Robbins' 1922 novel about boxing and life

Finger-prints Never Lie — A 1939 classic detective novel by John G. Brandon.

Freaks and Fantasies — Eerie tales by Tod Robbins, collaborator of Tod Browning on the film FREAKS.

Gadsby — A lipogram (a novel without the letter E). Ernest Vincent Wright's last work, published in 1939 right before his death.

Gelett Burgess Novels — *The Master of Mysteries, The White Cat, Two O'Clock Courage, Ladies in Boxes, Find the Woman, The Heart Line, The Picaroons* and *Lady Mechante*. Recently added is A Gelett Burgess Sampler, edited by Alfred Jan. All are introduced by Richard A. Lupoff.

Geronimo — S. M. Barrett's 1905 autobiography of a noble American.

Hake Talbot Novels — *Rim of the Pit, The Hangman's Handyman*. Classic locked room mysteries, with mapback covers by Gavin O'Keefe.

Hands Out of Hell and Other Stories — John H. Knox's eerie hallucinations

Hell is a City — William Ard's masterpiece.

Hollywood Dreams — A novel of Tinsel Town and the Depression by Richard O'Brien.

Hostesses in Hell and Other Stories — Russell Gray's most graphic stories

House of the Restless Dead — Strange and ominous tales by Hugh B. Cave.

I Stole $16,000,000 — A true story by cracksman Herbert E. Wilson.

Inclination to Murder — 1966 thriller by New Zealand's Harriet Hunter.

Invaders from the Dark — Classic werewolf tale from Greye La Spina.

J. Poindexter, Colored — Classic satirical black novel by Irvin S. Cobb.

Jack Mann Novels — Strange murder in the English countryside. *Gees' First Case, Nightmare Farm, Grey Shapes, The Ninth Life, The Glass Too Many, Her Ways Are Death, The Kleinert Case* and *Maker of Shadows*.

Jake Hardy — A lusty western tale from Wesley Tallant.

Jim Harmon Double Novels — *Vixen Hollow/Celluloid Scandal, The Man Who Made Maniacs/Silent Siren, Ape Rape/Wanton Witch, Sex Burns Like Fire/Twist Session, Sudden Lust/Passion Strip, Sin Unlimited/Harlot Master, Twilight Girls/Sex Institution*. Written in the early 60s and never reprinted until now.

Joel Townsley Rogers Novels and Short Stories — By the author of *The Red Right Hand: Once In a Red Moon, Lady With the Dice, The Stopped Clock, Never Leave My Bed*. Also two short story collections: *Night of Horror* and *Killing Time*.

John Carstairs, Space Detective — Arboreal Sci-fi by Frank Belknap Long

Joseph Shallit Novels — *The Case of the Billion Dollar Body, Lady Don't Die on My Doorstep, Kiss the Killer, Yell Bloody Murder, Take Your Last Look*. One of America's best 50's authors and a favorite of author Bill Pronzini.

Keller Memento — 45 short stories of the amazing and weird by Dr. David Keller.

Killer's Caress — Cary Moran's 1936 hardboiled thriller.

Lady of the Yellow Death and Other Stories — More stories by Wyatt Blassingame.

League of the Grateful Dead and Other Stories — Volume One in the Day Keene in the Detective Pulps series.

Library of Death — Ghastly tale by Ronald S. L. Harding, introduced by John Pelan

Malcolm Jameson Novels and Short Stories — *Astonishing! Astounding!, Tarnished Bomb, The Alien Envoy and Other Stories* and *The Chariots of San Fernando and Other Stories*. All introduced and edited by John Pelan or Richard A. Lupoff.

Man Out of Hell and Other Stories — Volume II of the John H. Knox weird pulps collection.

Marblehead: A Novel of H.P. Lovecraft — A long-lost masterpiece from Richard A. Lupoff. This is the "director's cut", the long version that has never been published before.

Mark of the Laughing Death and Other Stories — Shockers from the pulps by Francis James, introduced by John Pelan.

Master of Souls — Mark Hansom's 1937 shocker is introduced by weirdologist John Pelan.

Max Afford Novels — *Owl of Darkness, Death's Mannikins, Blood on His Hands, The Dead Are Blind, The Sheep and the Wolves, Sinners in Paradise* and *Two Locked Room Mysteries and a Ripping Yarn* by one of Australia's finest mystery novelists.

Money Brawl — Two books about the writing business by Jack Woodford and H. Bedford-Jones. Introduced by Richard A. Lupoff.

More Secret Adventures of Sherlock Holmes — Gary Lovisi's second collection of tales about the unknown sides of the great detective.

Muddled Mind: Complete Works of Ed Wood, Jr. — David Hayes and Hayden Davis deconstruct the life and works of the mad, but canny, genius.

Murder among the Nudists — A mystery from 1934 by Peter Hunt, featuring a naked Detective-Inspector going undercover in a nudist colony.

Murder in Black and White — 1931 classic tennis whodunit by Evelyn Elder.

Murder in Shawnee — Two novels of the Alleghenies by John Douglas: *Shawnee Alley Fire* and *Haunts.*

Murder in Silk — A 1937 Yellow Peril novel of the silk trade by Ralph Trevor.

My Deadly Angel — 1955 Cold War drama by John Chelton.

My First Time: The One Experience You Never Forget — Michael Birchwood — 64 true first-person narratives of how they lost it.

Mysterious Martin, the Master of Murder — Two versions of a strange 1912 novel by Tod Robbins about a man who writes books that can kill.

Norman Berrow Novels — *The Bishop's Sword, Ghost House, Don't Go Out After Dark, Claws of the Cougar, The Smokers of Hashish, The Secret Dancer, Don't Jump Mr. Boland!, The Footprints of Satan, Fingers for Ransom, The Three Tiers of Fantasy, The Spaniard's Thumb, The Eleventh Plague, Words Have Wings, One Thrilling Night, The Lady's in Danger, It Howls at Night, The Terror in the Fog, Oil Under the Window, Murder in the Melody, The Singing Room.* This is the complete Norman Berrow library of locked-room mysteries, several of which are masterpieces.

Old Faithful and Other Stories — SF classic tales by Raymond Z. Gallun.

Old Times' Sake — Short stories by James Reasoner from Mike Shayne Magazine.

One Dreadful Night — A classic mystery by Ronald S. L. Harding

Pair O' Jacks — A mystery novel and a diatribe about publishing by Jack Woodford

Perfect .38 — Two early Timothy Dane novels by William Ard. More to come.

Prince Pax — Devilish intrigue by George Sylvester Viereck and Philip Eldridge

Prose Bowl — Futuristic satire of a world where hack writing has replaced football as our national obsession, by Bill Pronzini and Barry N. Malzberg.

Red Light — The history of legal prostitution in Shreveport Louisiana by Eric Brock. Includes wonderful photos of the houses and the ladies.

Researching American-Made Toy Soldiers — A 276-page collection of a lifetime of articles by toy soldier expert Richard O'Brien.

Reunion in Hell — Volume One of the John H. Knox series of weird stories from the pulps. Introduced by horror expert John Pelan.

Ripped from the Headlines! — The Jack the Ripper story as told in the newspaper articles in the *New York* and *London Times.*

Rough Cut & New, Improved Murder — Ed Gorman's first two novels.

R.R. Ryan Novels — Freak Museum and The Subjugated Beast, two horror classics.

Ruby of a Thousand Dreams — The villain Wu Fang returns in this Roland Daniel novel.

Ruled By Radio — 1925 futuristic novel by Robert L. Hadfield & Frank E. Farncombe.

Rupert Penny Novels — *Policeman's Holiday, Policeman's Evidence, Lucky Policeman, Policeman in Armour, Sealed Room Murder, Sweet Poison, The Talkative Policeman, She had to Have Gas* and *Cut and Run* (by Martin Tanner.) Rupert Penny is the pseudonym of Australian Charles Thornett, a master of the locked room, impossible crime plot.

Sacred Locomotive Flies — Richard A. Lupoff's psychedelic SF story.

Sam — Early gay novel by Lonnie Coleman.

The Curse of Cantire — Classic 1939 novel of a family curse by Walter S. Masterman.

The Devil and the C.I.D. — Odd diabolic mystery by E.C.R. Lorac

The Devil Drives — An odd prison and lost treasure novel from 1932 by Virgil Markham.

The Devil of Pei-Ling — Herbert Asbury's 1929 tale of the occult.

The Devil's Mistress — A 1915 Scottish gothic tale by J. W. Brodie-Innes, a member of Aleister Crowley's Golden Dawn.

The Devil's Nightclub and Other Stories — John Pelan introduces some gruesome tales by Nat Schachner.

The Disentanglers — Episodic intrigue at the turn of last century by Andrew Lang

The Dog Poker Code — A spoof of *The Da Vinci Code* by D.B. Smithee.

The Dumpling — Political murder from 1907 by Coulson Kernahan.

The End of It All and Other Stories — Ed Gorman selected his favorite short stories for this huge collection.

The Fangs of Suet Pudding — A 1944 novel of the German invasion by Adams Farr

The Finger of Destiny and Other Stories — Edmund Snell's superb collection of weird stories of Borneo.

The Ghost of Gaston Revere — From 1935, a novel of life and beyond by Mark Hansom, introduced by John Pelan.

The Girl in the Dark — A thriller from Roland Daniel

The Gold Star Line — Seaboard adventure from L.T. Reade and Robert Eustace.

The Golden Dagger — 1951 Scotland Yard yarn by E. R. Punshon.

The Great Orme Terror — Horror stories by Garnett Radcliffe from the pulps

The Hairbreadth Escapes of Major Mendax — Francis Blake Crofton's 1889 boys' book.

The House That Time Forgot and Other Stories — Insane pulpitude by Robert F. Young

The House of the Vampire — 1907 poetic thriller by George S. Viereck.

The Illustrious Corpse — Murder hijinx from Tiffany Thayer

The Incredible Adventures of Rowland Hern — Intriguing 1928 impossible crimes by Nicholas Olde.

The Julius Caesar Murder Case — A classic 1935 re-telling of the assassination by Wallace Irwin that's much more fun than the Shakespeare version.

The Koky Comics — A collection of all of the 1978-1981 Sunday and daily comic strips by Richard O'Brien and Mort Gerberg, in two volumes.

The Lady of the Terraces — 1925 missing race adventure by E. Charles Vivian.

The Lord of Terror — 1925 mystery with master-criminal, Fantômas.

The Melamare Mystery — A classic 1929 Arsene Lupin mystery by Maurice Leblanc

The Man Who Was Secrett — Epic SF stories from John Brunner

The Man Without a Planet — Science fiction tales by Richard Wilson

The N. R. De Mexico Novels — Robert Bragg, the real N.R. de Mexico, presents *Marijuana Girl, Madman on a Drum, Private Chauffeur* in one volume.

The Night Remembers — A 1991 Jack Walsh mystery from Ed Gorman.

The One After Snelling — Kickass modern noir from Richard O'Brien.

The Organ Reader — A huge compilation of just about everything published in the 1971-1972 radical bay-area newspaper, *THE ORGAN*. A coffee table book that points out the shallowness of the coffee table mindset.

The Poker Club — Three in one! Ed Gorman's ground-breaking novel, the short story it was based upon, and the screenplay of the film made from it.

The Private Journal & Diary of John H. Surratt — The memoirs of the man who conspired to assassinate President Lincoln.

The Ramble House Mapbacks — Recently revised book by Gavin L. O'Keefe with color pictures of all the Ramble House books with mapbacks.

The Secret Adventures of Sherlock Holmes — Three Sherlockian pastiches by the Brooklyn author/publisher, Gary Lovisi.

The Shadow on the House — Mark Hansom's 1934 masterpiece of horror is introduced by John Pelan.

The Sign of the Scorpion — A 1935 Edmund Snell tale of oriental evil.

The Singular Problem of the Stygian House-Boat — Two classic tales by John Kendrick Bangs about the denizens of Hades.

The Smiling Corpse — Philip Wylie and Bernard Bergman's odd 1935 novel.

The Spider: Satan's Murder Machines — A thesis about Iron Man

The Stench of Death: An Odoriferous Omnibus by Jack Moskovitz — Two complete novels and two novellas from 60's sleaze author, Jack Moskovitz.

The Story Writer and Other Stories — Classic SF from Richard Wilson

The Strange Case of the Antlered Man — 1935 dementia from Edwy Searles Brooks

The Strange Thirteen — Richard B. Gamon's odd stories about Raj India.

The Technique of the Mystery Story — Carolyn Wells' tips about writing.

The Threat of Nostalgia — A collection of his most obscure stories by Jon Breen

The Time Armada — Fox B. Holden's 1953 SF gem.

The Tongueless Horror and Other Stories — Volume One of the series of short stories from the weird pulps by Wyatt Blassingame.

The Town from Planet Five — From Richard Wilson, two SF classics, *And Then the Town Took Off* and *The Girls from Planet 5*

The Tracer of Lost Persons — From 1906, an episodic novel that became a hit radio series in the 30s. Introduced by Richard A. Lupoff.

The Trail of the Cloven Hoof — Diabolical horror from 1935 by Arlton Eadie. Introduced by John Pelan.

The Triune Man — Mindscrambling science fiction from Richard A. Lupoff.

The Unholy Goddess and Other Stories — Wyatt Blassingame's first DTP compilation

The Universal Holmes — Richard A. Lupoff's 2007 collection of five Holmesian pastiches and a recipe for giant rat stew.

The Werewolf vs the Vampire Woman — Hard to believe ultraviolence by either Arthur M. Scarm or Arthur M. Scram.

The Whistling Ancestors — A 1936 classic of weirdness by Richard E. Goddard and introduced by John Pelan.

The White Owl — A vintage thriller from Edmund Snell

The White Peril in the Far East — Sidney Lewis Gulick's 1905 indictment of the West and assurance that Japan would never attack the U.S.

The Wizard of Berner's Abbey — A 1935 horror gem written by Mark Hansom and introduced by John Pelan.

The Wonderful Wizard of Oz — by L. Frank Baum and illustrated by Gavin L. O'Keefe

Through the Looking Glass — Lewis Carroll wrote it; Gavin L. O'Keefe illustrated it.

Time Line — Ramble House artist Gavin O'Keefe selects his most evocative art inspired by the twisted literature he reads and designs.

Tiresias — Psychotic modern horror novel by Jonathan M. Sweet.

Tortures and Towers — Two novellas of terror by Dexter Dayle.

Totah Six-Pack — Fender Tucker's six tales about Farmington in one sleek volume.

Tree of Life, Book of Death — Grania Davis' book of her life.

Triple Quest — An arty mystery from the 30s by E.R. Punshon.

Trail of the Spirit Warrior — Roger Haley's saga of life in the Indian Territories.

Two Kinds of Bad — Two 50s novels by William Ard about Danny Fontaine

Two Suns of Morcali and Other Stories — Evelyn E. Smith's SF tour-de-force

Ultra-Boiled — 23 gut-wrenching tales by our Man in Brooklyn, Gary Lovisi.

Up Front From Behind — A 2011 satire of Wall Street by James B. Kobak.

Victims & Villains — Intriguing Sherlockiana from Derham Groves.

Wade Wright Novels — *Echo of Fear, Death At Nostalgia Street, It Leads to Murder* and *Shadows' Edge*, a double book featuring *Shadows Don't Bleed* and *The Sharp Edge*.

Walter S. Masterman Novels — *The Green Toad, The Flying Beast, The Yellow Mistletoe, The Wrong Verdict, The Perjured Alibi, The Border Line, The Bloodhounds Bay, The Curse of Cantire* and *The Baddington Horror*. Masterman wrote horror and mystery, some introduced by John Pelan.

We Are the Dead and Other Stories — Volume Two in the Day Keene in the Detective Pulps series, introduced by Ed Gorman. When done, there may be 11 in the series.

Welsh Rarebit Tales — Charming stories from 1902 by Harle Oren Cummins

West Texas War and Other Western Stories — by Gary Lovisi.

What If? Volume 1, 2 and 3 — Richard A. Lupoff introduces three decades worth of SF short stories that should have won a Hugo, but didn't.

When the Batman Thirsts and Other Stories — Weird tales from Frederick C. Davis.

Whip Dodge: Man Hunter — Wesley Tallant's saga of a bounty hunter of the old West.

Win, Place and Die! — The first new mystery by Milt Ozaki in decades. The ultimate novel of 70s Reno.

Writer 1 and 2 — A magnus opus from Richard A. Lupoff summing up his life as writer.

You'll Die Laughing — Bruce Elliott's 1945 novel of murder at a practical joker's English countryside manor.

RAMBLE HOUSE
Fender Tucker, Prop.   Gavin L. O'Keefe, Graphics
www.ramblehouse.com   fender@ramblehouse.com
228-826-1783   10329 Sheephead Drive, Vancleave MS 39565

www.ingramcontent.com/pod-product-compliance
Lightning Source LLC
Chambersburg PA
CBHW030334030726
47499CB00003B/766